I0573552

The Callings

C.C. Spicer

Cadmus Publishing
www.cadmuspublishing.com

Published by Cadmus Publishing
www.cadmuspublishing.com
Port Angeles, WA

ISBN: 978-1-63751-280-7

Table of Contents

Author's Note

I don't care frankly what people think. I do what I like. I'm a dreamer.

DEDICATION

For,
Family

FORWARD

Fate- Something that's destined to happen no matter who or what tries to intervene. That's where she comes in. Yuki. To the blind eye she could be a killer, drug dealer, prostitute, friend or foe. She is any and everybody she needs to be in order to fulfill Fates Callings. It will be successful. Yuki has a highly elite trained, gorgeous and most important, deadly, team of women. All Japanese. She is the head and they make up the body. Usually Yuki doesn't personally fulfill fates obligations but this specific job has intrigued her. Its been an existing problem for a while. A lot of the fate Seekers were killed in the pursuit during this specific job.

This group of assassins has been in existence for centuries. Some believe that they are just myth or some type of urban legend because of the things they are supposed to be able to do. They have gifts. Above any and all living creatures, the fate seekers are at the top of the food chain. The mission, Yuki's current situation, Ethan McDonald, a senator for the State of Texas. Fate decided it was his time, but with his money and influences he decided not to accept.

Wrong decision.

The reason Yuki had to complete the job was because if all else fails, she doesn't. Ethan knew the Seekers were on his trail. His security detail already killed a few of them. But this particular weekend he slipped... Ethan was on a vacation on some far away island off the coast of Hawaii. It was beautiful. The sun was at its highest in the sky. The water, crystal clear that you could see tot the bottom. Nothing but nature behind him. He decided to leave his security detail behind thinking Fate didn't travel.

Deadly mistake.

Swimming through some choppy waters, Yuki glided like a snake. She sensed Ethan's aroma as she neared. Navy Seal style. slightly she peeked her head above the water. She spotted the man of the hour. Ethan McDonald. He was laid out with woman that Yuki was for sure wasn't his wife, sunbathing. Yuki was about a mile from shore and noticed all of this. A gift, vision. She swam closer in pursuit not coming up for air, another gift, gills in the water.

Ethan's lady friend noticed Yuki coming off the water heading for the sand. "Ethan, baby!? I thought this was our island for the weekend." The blonde hottie said reaching for a towel because she was in the nude.

In a heavy Texan accent he replied. "Now lady, I done tol' you, this is my her' island foe' the weekend, ya' hear."

"Yes, Big Daddy, but who's her?" She pointed.

Ethan looked in the direction the lady pointed and almost lost everything he'd just ate. "Sheeit! We gotta' get gone." He said grabbing his towel running for the woods.

He ran through the tree's leaving his date behind on the sand. Crashing in-between the twigs and branches of the jungle, he ran for his life. Sweat coursed down his face from the exhaustion of being out of shape. Yuki walked past the woman in the direction Ethan sprinted to. She knew he had nowhere to go. He was dropped off by boat and it wouldn't return until Sunday. She did her homework. It was Friday.

Ethan was sprinting. Yuki could still see him even though he was a good distance on front of her. He stopped at a waterfall, a log was in the river that led to the other side. he decided crossing it or running along side the river taking him deeper into the jungle. Yuki watched. Crawling on the log, Ethan made it to the other side. Yuki smiled, "Bold move." she uttered. If the log would have bulged, Ethan would have fallen over the waterfall and into the ocean.

An idea formed in Ethan's head. Grabbing another slightly jagged log, he tried to pry the other log that was embedded in the river in an attempt to take the path away. "Yeeha!" He celebrated after successfully prying the log watching it roll with the flow of the river. He then continued to run.

"I had enough of this." Yuki said more to herself but out loud.

She ran full speed in pursuit. Ethan was pretty far, but with a squint of her eye she could zoom all the way in and pinpoint his exact location. Within seconds Yuki made it to the river that Ethan minutes. She smiled. "Humans." Then uttered after realizing what Ethan attempted to do.

She took a few steps back, then glided over the river with a foot to spare on the landing. "Ahhh!" Yuki heard a scream on the distance. With a squint of her eyelids she noticed a jagged rock tore Ethan's foot wide open. Yuki's mouth watered. She could taste fate. ignoring the pain, Ethan continued to run. His moves were fueled and driven only by instinct.

Thunder roared. A bolt of lightning struck. It landed directly in front of Ethan stopping him dead in his tracks. Almost instantly the ground was slick and muddy from the quick shower. Any hopes he had on escaping evaporated when Yuki appeared before him in an all black form fitting body suit dripping wet with snake-like eyes. "Sumimasen." She apologized with a slight bow.

"W-wait, what?" Ethan was confused. He didn't understand the Japanese language.

In a few quick but precise movements, Ethan's pulse slowed, his ribs cracked sending him into spasms as his knees buckled. On the ground he was gripping his neck trying to keep it attached to his head. With the shuriken Yuki pulled out her hair then out of his neck in one hand she gave Ethan an option. Her other hand was empty as she put both palms up.

"Erabeto." She told him to choose his fate. He looked confused. Ethan didn't understand. Yuki lift her left palm, "Hidari," then her right, "Migi?"

Guessing that Yuki was giving him a way out because she said everything with a smile, he picked the left hand which was empty. As fast as Ethan picked the left, Yuki turned it around palms down and jabbed it into his chest instantly stopping his heart. "Jamata Gambatte." Yuki said, letting him know she'll see him later and good luck.

After a few customary bows, Yuki left him where he stood, on his knees in a dead mans stare. After a quick flight, Yuki was back at the Fate Seeker's mansion. She called a meeting. Not wasting anytime she began with her lecture in front of multiple seekers.

"It's time to change. Change is constant in this new world order. The humans are coming up with new gadgets or what not and we need to adapt. I have an idea for a new Seeker that nobody would even care to look at. I shouldn't have to be the one to clean up after any of you but here I am. For that reason I have the perfect type of person. Tomorrow, Ill go hunting. Arigato Konbawa." Yuki finished, thanking them and giving them the evening greeting.

CHAPTER 1

WASHINGTON D.C.

Hot and steamy. Mean and muggy. It was the type of weather that made you angry. Well at least that what most peoples assumptions were when they noticed your face. Tight jaws and squinted eyes were nearly every persons facial expression in the neighborhood against the heat.

Ninety-five degrees.

It was a scorcher. The humidity was what really messed with your head. Sweat beads attacked the forehead of many as soon as they crossed the threshold of any door...

"I DON'T KNOW WHAT I WAS THINKING. I KNEW THIS WAS TOO GOOD TO BE TRUE, BUT SHIT. IT WAS RIGHT THERE IN MY GRASP FOR THE TAKING. ANY MAN WOULD'VE FELT TEMPTED. WHAT WAS I SUPPOSED TO DO? ALL IN ALL I SHOULD HAVE KNOWN. IM NEVER THAT LUCKY." Solo pondered.

...There Solo was, posted on the corner of his neighborhood block in an attempt to hail a cab, nearly an impossible task in the area. Still, he stood in hopes of a willing driver. he had a few things on his agenda, but time was not on his side. The clock was ticking but he wasn't late, yet. If a ride wasn't hailed, Solo would miss his interview for a job opening. He was not trying to go back home to hear his mothers rants.

Seemed as if lady luck was on solo's side today as his silent prayer was answered. A limo style Lincoln town car pulled directly in front of him. It wasn't stretched. He leaned over trying to peek inside. The passenger window descended. A beautiful, jaw dropping Japanese woman was in clear view. "Konichiwa!" She spoke happily.

With a screw face look of confusion, Solo responded, "What!?" Not disrespectful, only in reaction to not understanding her language.

It was foreign, but at the same time sounded sexy in his ears with the melody of the accent. "I was speaking to you," She translated, "but do you need a ride somewhere? It looks like you're in desperate need," She asked with a smile that just seemed to brighten his face.

"Hell yea I need a ride!" Solo responded excited and anxious at the same time as he quickly got in the backseat. The a/c attacked his face. "Damn. This air feel good as shit, I'm Solo by the way and thank you."

"You're very welcome, it's my pleasure. I'm Yuki." She responded licking her lips, flirtaciously.

The car was polished and well detailed inside and out. Wood grained accessories and pure gold trim were everywhere throughout. Solo began to actually notice the cleanliness of the vehicle and started to question if Yuki expected some type of currency exchange because his funds were on the skinny side.

At most he had fifteen dollars for transportation, there and back. Sitting in the car, Solo began to maneuver his body getting comfortable. The seats were cooled and oddly had massage switches on the arm rest which he didn't hesitate to try.

"This some nice shit here," Solo said more to himself looking around at the possibilities. Noticing more massage buttons he hit one. "OH SHIT! That's what I'm talkin' bout." His eyes rolled to the back of his head as he enjoyed the different combinations it had to offer.

He looked like a child with a new toy. Yuki was eyeing him smiling. "You having fun over there?" Solo just looked at her, raised his eyebrows and returned her smile without comment so she continued. "So, Mr. Solo, where are we headed?"

He was so in awe of the car and all it had to offer, he slightly forgot about today's agenda. Snapping back to reality he started to speak. "Oh shit, I nearly forgot. I'm headed to uhhh,damn, hold on," Solo shuffled through his pockets for the address, "found it! It's a suite on Pennsylvania Ave, the 700 block." He said reading from the crumbled flyer.

Solo was in search of obtaining a labor job that was advertized. It offered $12.00 a hour for entry level. Valerie, his mother, was on his case about gaining some type of employment. He was a recent high school graduate and college wasn't in his thoughts. he wasn't the best hustler. Selling drugs was a common outlet in his neighborhood for money, but he could never level up like the urban street legends and surpass the corner boy status.

Pulling up in front of an office building, Solo was ready to put on his best "Hampton Boy" act in an attempt to impress the employer into hiring him. Yuki gave off this mysterious look that seemed to draw Solo in. Shaking off random thoughts, Solo spoke, "Thanks for the ride, Ms. lady. I really 'preciate it." He said extending his hand to pay her with a ten dollar bill.

Yuki looked at the money and waved it off. "Here, take this." She handed him a metallic black business card with a red blood-like drop on the center of it with a number below, "call me if you want a real job."

Solo was curious, he wanted to ask a few questions about the job offering, but time wasn't on his side. The interview he had scheduled was near. He accepted the card, it pinched him causing a thin line of blood. "Shit!" he sucked his finger. With his right hand he extended his arm for a handshake.

Yuki pulled him close with the strength of a man. 'DAMN, LIKE THE MATRIX!' Solo thought before Yuki forced a kiss on his lips. he felt her tongue wrestling down his throat and his eyes widen during the kiss. 'DO HER TONGUE GOT SLITS?' He thought but was lost in the ecstasy of the moment and just went with it. It was his first kiss from a foreign woman and he enjoyed the feeling of it.

It felt so good that his manhood started to rise through his slacks. Yuki broke the kiss and pushed him back. "Call me, for work that is, " Her window slowly rose with her last testament, "Ja Mata." Looking back at Yuki with a puzzled face as she spoke more of her native language before the window reached the top she told him, "It means, Ill see you next time."

Standing in the middle of the block with a lot of questions and in a state of confusion, Solo shook it off then headed to the building. "Time to put on." Solo said brushing himself off imaginary dust, ironing wrinkles from his shirt.

CHAPTER 2

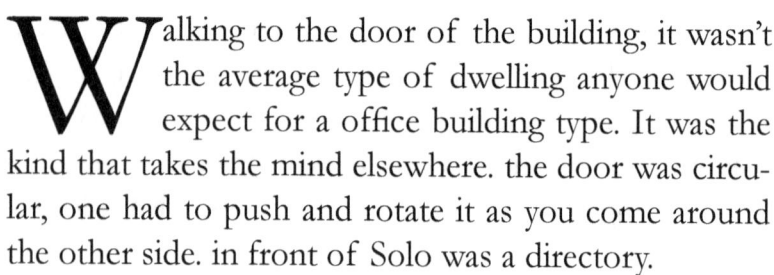

Walking to the door of the building, it wasn't the average type of dwelling anyone would expect for a office building type. It was the kind that takes the mind elsewhere. the door was circular, one had to push and rotate it as you come around the other side. in front of Solo was a directory.

The place had a museum feeling to it. 'FANCY' he thought looking up from the directory. The sounds coming from the area were those of elevator music, but everywhere. 'WEIRD' he shrugged his shoulders and slid his finger back down the directory. Locating the floor he needed to be on, Solo turned around in search of the stairs. He didn't like elevators. The stairs were different from what he was used to. They were wide and flat Asian style steps that wrapped the circumference of the building. Nothing in the building made sense in his opinion. Still, he needed a job so he continued to walk and made it to the suite he was searching for.

There was a door, he debated knocking but decided against it and went straight in and looked around. All he had the chances to do was glance before the reception-ist was on his line quick. "Uh,Sir, Can I help you?" She asked popping gum

. 'GHETTO ASS.' Solo thought but kept it together as he responded in his best Hampton voice. "You sure can. I'm here for an interview." He smiled, so sure of himself.

With the phone cord wrapped around her fingers she looked at Solo and spoke into the phone, "Hold on, Girl," Confusion etched her face at his request as she shuffled through some papers in front of her. "Uh Sir, What time was your interview scheduled for?" She asked not even looking up from her files.

"2:00 pm sharp." Solo said looking at his watch and saw it read 2:04 pm. No worries on his face.

"Ooo-okay," She dragged it out with a smile that quickly disappeared, "Well, it's 3:05 and my supervisor is gone out on errands, shit, he might be gone for the day." She said matterfactly.

"What! You trippin' like big shoes," Solo said drop-ping the preppy act,"My watch aint wrong shawty." He said pulling out his phone to confirm. He shook his head as he slowly lowered it. The receptionist was right. He felt stupid.

She must had known it too as she blew a bubble then popped her gum loud enough to bring Solo out of his daze. "Sorry." She chewed.

Irritated he reached over the desk, she leaned back alittle startled at his motions as she tried to avoid his hands not knowing his intentions. Solo grabbed a handful of candy out of the dish and stuffed it into his pockets. "Thank you for nothing, Stupid." and left.

CHAPTER 3

Exiting the building Solo was a little agitated. He didn't believe what had just happened.

"How my watch do some shit like that?" He cursed himself.

The streets were busy. Rush hour. The worst time of the day to travel. Shoulder to shoulder traffic was what he was experiencing in the train subway station. He wasn't even on the train yet and the platform was over-crowded. Youthful children were released from school and were everywhere along with the people coming from work.

Loud and crazy was the best way to describe their actions. One guy stepped on Solo's shoes!

A violation. The guy looked back knowing and well aware of what he did, he eyed Solo up and down then looked back forward not saying a word as if nothing happened. 'THE DISRESPECT OF THIS GUY.' Solo shook his head. He had on a casual outfit on and the guy must had assumed Solo was going to accept that.

Tapping the guy on his shoulder to grab his attention, he spoke, "My man, my man,"

The guy turned to face Solo with a frown o his face and swelled up, "What Chump! You want a problem?"

Solo already had a temper that he was working on and he was dealing with not even getting a chance to get that job, still he tried to be respectful, "Not looking for a problem, but I wasn't sure if you was aware that you stepped on my loafers." He said calmly and articulately.

Turning his nose up, the guy responded. "Fuck dem' loafers!"

SMACK!

Solo blanked out. If the scene would had been a cartoon, that would've been the part when steam blew out his ears before Solo hauled off and put hands on the guy. The strike knocked the guy off balance.

"Ahhh, damn, Cuz." He fell onto another passenger behind him.

"Get off me!!!" the passenger said pushing him back toward Solo as he held his cheek.

SMACK!

Solo hit him again. This time he fell. The guy had no idea he was hit again until he felt his back on the cold platform as he looked at the lights of the ceiling. Stepping over the guy, Solo headed to the approaching train mumbling to himself, "Fuck my loafers, huh? Nah fuck yo' face."

As the doors closed, a couple of kids ran to the guy on the ground laughing and pointing. "You got smacked out!" Then went through his pockets relieving him of all valuables.

He tried to stop them but he was still seeing stars. With a final punch to the chin, he was asleep and snoring as the train pulled off. Getting off the train, Solo had to face the music as he walked toward his house. Valerie had been calling to get an update, but he ignored the calls. He even debated staying outside until later to avoid her but he had to change his attire. Walking past a school, he decided to pick his little brother up since he knew his mother didn't come as of yet and wanted to save her the trip and possible gain some cool points. The good deed might take some of the tongue lashing away that he was sure to receive.

"Solo!!" Riley screamed in joy at the sight of his brother, "What are doing here?"

"Coming to get you, Big Time, duh, you ite?"

"Uh huh."

" How was school? you learn sumtin'?"

"Of course. I did good today too," Riley said reaching in his backpack , "Look!" he tried to show Solo some of his work he did today.

"Later, later, Bigtime." Solo said giving his brother a playful nuggy as hey walked home.

Riley ran the rest of the way after getting loose and Valerie came into view. She had the look of shock noticing Riley running her way until she saw Solo, then only did her facial features lighten up. Coming into arm distance Solo hugged his mother, kissing her on the cheek. "Sup' Ma, thought I save you the trip and get Riley for you." He said, then tried to walk past. That attempt was gated.

"So baby, how did it go?" Valerie asked, "look at you, my baby so handsome," She complimented his attire and presence. Solo stopped dead in his tracks and blew a sigh. He shook his head in defeat. "I didn't get it." He said hoping she accepted the brief answer as he tried to keep it moving.

Valerie was persistent. Every step he took, she took two to narrow the gap. "So, what happened Baby?" She asked grabbing his arm in an attempt to slow him down. "I know you could do the job with all them muscles.

Riley stayed and watched the whole encounter. He looked as if he was just as interested as he stood beside Valerie waiting on a explanation. "I know how this about to sound but I don't know what happened," He nervously started to scratch his head, "but my watch randomly stopped working and fell a hour behind so I was late." Solo said looking away.

Valerie's facial expression went from sorrow to irritation as she listened. "Damn Dummy!" She said popping him in the back of his head.

As she past Solo, Riley jumped in the air popping Solo in the same spot their mother just did. "Dummy!" Riley ran. Solo tried to grab him but riley screamed, "Maaaa!" making Valerie turn around.

"Leave him alone! You should have ran your hind parts to that damn interview." Valerie said walking with Riley close by as he licked his tongue at his big brother.

Solo put his fist to his own eye giving Riley a warning as he walked behind them into the house. He walked to his room to get out of the cloths he had on. Emptying his pockets, he looked at the black card and pondered, "A real job, huh?' then tossed it on the dresser. Looking in his hiding spot, he grabbed the last few baggies of drugs he had in attempt to make a few dollars. His pockets were hurting and screaming "Somebody help" so he put on some cargo shorts and a tank top with a pair of Nike Air Max's. outside was the next destination.

The projects where Solo lived had every type of hustler you could think of. There was no age restriction to the grind. Everyone had different and the same products. Some sold candy, dinner plates, hair do's and everything in-between. If you didn't want to leave the projects, somebody had the bootleg hook up for the low. Solo's "hook up" was crack-cocaine. He didn't like to sell it, but he had to do what he had to survive. It was the best in his neighborhood. At least that's what he told everyone. He never smoked it, cooked it, or anything in that category as far as production. He only sold it, as is. he headed around different areas of the 'hood in search of potential customers.

All he ended of finding were different friends in their own circle of friends. Coming around another building, posted up, well sitting up as their feet dangled off the brick wall sat his men. His circle. Teddy and Onyx. These were some big fellas. There was no other way to describe the massive men. Solo was considered small compared to them even with his 5.9 frame and muscular toned body. Teddy and Onyx were about six feet and 270lbs solid. They were great in high school football, but loved the streets more. Academics were not a passion.

"What's up, Solo?" Teddy spoke,

"I see you still fluffy and cuddly."He said walking up on him giving dap, then extending the greeting to his other friend. "Onyx, what it do, Champ!"

"Same shit, Playboy. How da' interview go?" Onyx asked.

Solo shook his head. He was still a little embarrassed about how his day went. "Forget that, it was all bad. Do ya'll got some work?" He asked fishing, referring to drugs, really trying to change the subject.

"Nah', we finished. We just chillin' now." Teddy answered.

"Good, 'cause if ya'll did I was about to step off on ya'll," Solo said dead serious. "I'm broke as shit and aint got time for no breakdown shit." Solo finished.

"Damn Homes, Ol' petty ass." Onyx said throwing a little rock hitting Solo on the top of his head.

"Ow' Fool!" Solo rubbed his head, "I'm fucked up Bruh', Ma dukes on my top about getting a job and helping out with some doe."

"Sounds personal." Teddy said lighting a blunt.

"And emotional." Onyx countered.

"Tryna smoke?" Teddy asked.

Reaching for the blunt Solo shook his head, "And ya'll call me petty."

Chilling came natural. they smoked and enjoyed each others presence. They were high as the nearest cloud. Something didn't feel right. There was an eerie silence.

SKRRRRR!

Bright lights!

Out of nowhere the jump outs tried to trap them off. "One time!"

Solo was the quickest and the first to run. Onyx and Teddy ran after they heard the universal call on the sighting of the police. They were big, but fast as well. The police never had a chance once they made it to the middle of the projects and split up. There were too many cuts and hideouts for any resident with alil' speed to get caught. Solo high tailed back in the direction of his house. He was sweating profusely from the heat and the all out sprint. making it back to his door, he dusted himself off and caught his breath before entering his apartment.

Crossing the entrance, the a/c hit him and it felt so good. The front room area was the only space with air because it was a window unit. Whenever Valerie went upstairs, so did the air. Going into the kitchen, Valerie was eyeing Solo as he moved toward the fridge. "Boy! I know you not in my icebox with them dirty hands."

'ICEBOX?' He thought of the meaning, then realized.

"My bad." He said closing the door with a carton of Strawberry Melon Minute Maid already in his hand.

He poured a cup, leaving it on the countertop after he drank it's contents, then headed upstairs. "And when you come back downstairs here them dishes is gonna' be waiting on you!" Valerie screamed at his back."Lazy self".

Solo went to his room. Panicking, he was checking to see if his stash was still between his legs. "Please, please," He said frantically taking his pants off and shaking them out.

To his sad realization only two small baggies fell out with the wrapper that was supposed to hold them all. When he noticed that, he lowered his head in defeat. He knew it was over. To to be sure, Solo tip-toed back down the stairs looking at the carpet only all the way to the kitchen. Nothing. He came up empty, "Fuck!"

Solo whispered, but loud enough for Valerie to hear and grabbed her attention.

"Solo! Put some damn cloths on," She screamed on him, "with them little ass underwear. Who you think you is, Magic Mike?" Going back upstairs, in his room he put his clothes back on. On the the dresser he noticed the black card that the pretty Asian woman gave him earlier. The red dot was now glowing. "What the fu--?" The marijuana he smoked had him delirious. So he thought.

He was now questioning what was in that blunt Teddy and Onyx had him smoking. Moving closer to the card it seemed to be getting brighter and more enticing. Solo picked it up, and turned it around. The number was glowing. "Shit!" He rubbed his eyes, looked at the card and shrugged his shoulders."Why not?" He called.

"Konbanwa." A foreign voice answered the phone.

It sounded like the language Yuki spoke to him earlier. The melody of it had him hypnotized. He assumed it was some sort of greeting.

"Hello?!" Solo spoke. It was a natural response that came to mind. He figured it was a universal phrase but his guess was wrong.

"Chotto Matte." The voice responded, then silence. Solo was lost in the language barrier and the silence was now deafening. "Hello...hello?"

A few moments later another lady came to the phone. "Ello? ow mae help you?" came through the phone in broken English. Guessing she was asking, "How could she help" Solo gave her the only name he knew.

"Yuki."

"Tumarow, San jini, okay?"

"Huh? what?" After a sigh, she responded. "tumarrow three o'clock, okay." Click. She was gone.

CHAPTER 4

Solo didn't know what to think of the conversation he had earlier. After hanging out out in the house for about a hour, Yuki flooded his thoughts. All he knew was that he didn't have anything to lose by calling her tomorrow.

It seemed like it was some sort of professional type of work. He just hoped he was capable of completing the job. After hanging the cloths up that he tossed to the side earlier in search of his product, he fell back on his bed to relax. The bed was full sized. Nothing special. Let him tell it, it was "soft as a baby's bottom." He smiled basking in its glory.

Solo flicked on his television. He just recently brought it from one of the neighborhoods hustlers a couple of days ago for the low. It was a 60 inch off brand model flat screen. It didn't have any of the wall mounts when he purchased it, so he had no choice but to lean it against the wall on his dresser.

Living in the projects, the only option was to get it how you lived. To not comply meant the next man would run up on your come up and take it. No worries from Solo, he didn't take any nonsense from anyone. Everyone in his hood knew he wasn't the best hustler, but also knew he want no punk. Flipping through channels, Solo heard a constant sound hitting his window. It sounded like rocks or small pebbles were being thrown at it.

Walking to the window he noticed his on and off girlfriend. She was waving for him to come outside. Valerie didn't really care for her too much. She felt that when it comes to his girlfriend he becomes imperceptible to everything and she takes advantage of his feelings. They lost their virginity to one another in grade school but Valerie still know her son could do better than anyone in the neighborhood.

"Ebony, what the hell!?" He swung the door wide, "Why you throwing rocks at my damn window!."

"Why you aint answerin' da phone?" She countered with her hand on hip, then she tried her best to peek around him, "Who you got in there anyway?" She asked, already accusing with her tone.

That was one of their many problems. Trust. Ebony was insecure and thought Solo could have any girl in the world the way they responded to him. "Girl back up! Aint nobody in here. You know my moms home and she aint goin' for that shit." Solo defended.

"Whatever." She replied rolling her eyes.

Solo walked up on her looking around, nervously. He didn't forget he ran from the police earlier and they could've still been lurking the area. Thinking about it to himself, he figured the officers probably picked his stash up after the pursuit was over. Surveying with his eyes he finally had the second to finally get a full look at Ebony, she was gorgeous in his eyes. "Dayum' Girl, you know you sexy right?" She blushed.

Ebony had her hair in four tightly braided, french braids that came down her back. Her eyes were hazel, she stood 5'2, redbone in complexion,B cup sized breasts and a nice bubble rear end. Solo licked his lips in awe. She smiled noticing his lustful gaze. Quickly shutting down anything in that department she spoke, "Uh uh, Boy. I know dat' look. I'm on my cycle right now so..."

That statement in itself was enough to change his smile into a stink face of disgust. "Damn, you sure do know how to ruin a wet dream." Solo retorted.

"Awwww, poor Baby, come mer'," She teased reaching out for him, "Lets go out somewhere. I got my mother's car." ebony suggested.

He shrugged. "Shid' why not, aint got shit else to do."Solo said remembering his stash was now with the wind.

She was all smiles.

Walking down the sidewalk, Solo kicked a soda can that was in his path. Ebony was close beside him with not space between them. Looking around the neighborhood, it would look crazy to the outsiders riding by. To the residents, it's all they had to call home. Kids ran up and down the streets turning everything into a new toy.

Solo didn't know where they were headed but he hoped Ebony knew he as broke. If not, she would soon find out. Hitting her car alarm, Solo laughed unintentionally.

"What's so damn funny?" She asked looking him up and down.

"He looked toward the car then back at her, "What the hell dis' joint got an alarm for?"

Ebony's mother had a old model Kia, it definitely had seen better days. It was grey with slight factory tints and two missing hubcaps. The tail-lights had red tape on it giving the illusion it wasn't broke. To top it off, the front hood didn't close all the way due to an accident years ago.

"Shut up! You cant complain when you out here beatin' your feet!" She said defending her mother's car.

"Not for long." He mumbled.

Pulling off, Solo noticed Teddy and Onyx in the same spot that they just ran from earlier. They noticed him at the same time and the both of them jumped off the wall jogging in the direction of the car. Ebony blew a sigh as they neared. Inside she was heated, especially because the light was red and she couldn't pull off on them. Both back doors opened at the same time.

The car was already small so when the two massive men jumped in, it looked like they were in a Flintstone car how long to the ground it sank. It had no space for a pothole or speed bump.

"Oh hell nah', ya'll big asses gonna make my tires burst!" She spat.

Solo looked back at his friends ignoring Ebony's outburst, "Sup' wit ya'll?" He inquired.

"Shit, bored. Where ya'll going?"Teddy asked, "We tryna get out the 'hood for a minute."

Ebony interjected. "I don't care what ya'll tryna do! We goin out." She protested.

"Chill Lil' Evil, I got gas money and a few dollars foe my man. I know he broke. Them peoples picked up his stash. It was like a candy trail of coke." Onyx said, giving Ebony twenty dollars for her tank.

Solo sat there tight faced. Onyx just confirmed his suspicions about his stash. "Where was we goin' anyway?" Soli diverted.

"Tsst," She smacked her teeth, "I don't know."

Teddy saw a sign, "Aye, look!."He said pointing."Its a carnival at the mall out Princes George's County, we could slide thru' that joint."

Solo looked behind his seat to make eye contact with his friends to get a better understanding. If he was going to go to the carnival he needed confirmation on the fee's. "Ya'll treating, right?"

"We got you?" Onyx said looking at Teddy.

Solo looked over at his girl. Ebony just ignored his stares, but continued to drive. He didn't mind the carnival, really it was a good pastime until tomorrow so he could check out the job and what it entails. At the carnival they actually had a good time. It took their minds away from the everyday nonsense of the urban life. Blending in with crowd, they blew smoke throughout, all but Ebony, who didn't indulge, as they went ride to ride.

Teddy even sold a few bags from the aroma it left floating in the air. Solo was happy because Ebony was. She was smiling and having a good time. He knew she only had the rest of the week to chill before she had to go back to school.

Ebony was in her second year at the University of New York. So really, in all actuality, this was their last date before the semester began and she had to head back up north.

It was closing time. The sun went down and the starts were out. "Don't see this in the city." Solo said as Ebony looked at the sky.

The scene was beautiful. Solo and Ebony was walking holding each others hand enjoying the sights. In front of them, above and around everything was colorful from the lights attached to the rides, to the people wearing lit up clothes and gadgets. The vibes were nice.

The moment was short lived. Teddy and Onyx reminded Solo of their presence as they both came between them breaking their embrace. "Nah', Lover boy, aint none of dat shit,"Teddy said. "People gonna think me and Onyx some type of couple, we all walking together."

"What's wrong wit' being gay?" Ebony protested.

"Aint shit wrong wit' it. Whatever floats ur' boat I don't give no shits about, "Teddy answered."Long as it aint me being placed in that scenario."

Onyx reached for Teddy's hand, grabbing it, and started to swing it while skipping. "Aww Baby, you ashamed of us?"

solo laughed as Teddy snatched his hand away pushing Onyx back and began wrestling and play fighting. Everyone laughed as they continued to walk. The night was young but Solo's day was nearing a end. He had plans for tomorrow.

CHAPTER 5

NEXT DAY

S olo woke up to the smell of bacon and hash browns. He knew it was more but that was the scent that attacked his nostrils waking him up. He got out the bed and fell straight on his back. "Riley!!!" He screamed getting back up.

He kicked his little brother's Tonka truck out the way as he limped to the bathrrom. He washed his face, brushed his teeth then headed downstairs to see what was on the menu.

Valerie smiled greeting him, "Good Morning Sleepy head?"

"Sup' Ma, it smell good in here, what's the occasion?"

"It's the morning. You eat a good breakfast, then get up outta here to find a damn job," She said placing the plate of food in front of him,"and I had a dream that you will find gainful employment. But when you finish eating take them with you." She nodded, pointing with her head.

Looking in the direction his mother nodded, he saw Teddy and Onyx with a plate in their laps with their faces cleaning the contents of it on the couch. "Damn." He didn't know how he missed their presence.

"Watch your mouth at my table," Valerie pointed the wooden spork she used to stir the eggs.

How the apartment was laid out, Solo would pass the living room before entering the kitchen. Following his nose in a smell pursuit, his tunnel vision activated leaving him oblivious to his surroundings.

After Solo ate, he went upstairs to take a quick shower while his friends played the PlayStation. Madden was their choice. He made it too the top of the steps and wondered when did his friends get in the house or if the even went home the night before.

'WHATEVER.' He chalked it up, his memory was clouded.

Heading to his room, the black card was now glowing again, but it was continuous, like a pulse of light. He walked to the dresser and picked the card up. Under the number it now had a message:

(THREE O'CLOCK)

It was in bold letters.

"What the --?" He dropped the card, stared at it for a moment, then snapped out of his trance picking the card back up that appeared to be normal again. "I gots to be trippin'." He told himself and headed to the shower.

Putting on some fresh fits for today, Sol stopped to observe himself in the mirror, posing. "You sexy beast you." After putting together the final touches to todays look he exited the room Opening his door, Solo saw his little brother sitting crossed legged in the middle of the hallway smiling in a full-size one-z.

"What you over there grinning for, Punk?" Solo asked.

Riley giggled. "Didn't you summon me, Big bro?" He asked then jumped up from the floor. Riley then threw the football he had hidden behind his back with all his strength. Unaware of it coming, it hit Solo in the center of his stomach knocking the wind out him.

Solo started to give chase, but after only three to four steps a thin line of dental floss tied from the rail to the door tripped him up.

"Ow! Shit!" He cursed as he fell and landed on his stomach, again.

Riley had an uncontrollable laugh and ran toward the stairs, "Who the Punk now!? He said skipping two steps at a time. Solo jumped up and ran behind him.

By the time Solo caught up to him, Riley was wrapped around their mother's leg licking his tongue out, tight eyed.

'I GOT YOUR BAD ASS.' Solo thought to himself as Teddy and Onyx got up from the couch following him out.

Leaving the apartment Teddy and Onyx were on his heels. Solo looked around, it felt like they were far removed from any kind of civilization. From the outside looking in, people might had thought no place was lonelier, drearier, no more intimidating in terms of complete isolation from the surrounding neighborhoods.

"Welcome to the projects." Solo said out loud for no specific reason.

"There he go again." Teddy head nodded towards Solo.

'Yea I know, I heard his ass, always in his own world." Onyx countered.

Solo turned around. "Ya'll know I could hear ya'll, right?"

"That's what we be like." Teddy said laughing, dapping Onyx up.

Solo had plans for today. It was one that was of real importance. That was to call that number and let everything else fall into place behind that. Getting in contact with Yuki was priority. He wondered what type of job she had to offer. Really it didn't matter, he definitely didn't care. All he wanted was to make some ends.

They headed to the basketball court, Teddy made a few transactions on the way. Onyx decided to fire up a blunt. Solo didn't want to, but the pressure of his friends made him hit it a few times. He didn't want to get too high, just buzzed. He only had an hour before it would be time to make the call.

Insanity.

It's the same story every time he smoke with his friends. To expect a different result when doing the same things. It's never just one blunt.

By the time they reached the court, Solo was high out his mind. He had cotton mouth and became very observant. The smallest things caught his eye and became noticeable. He began to zoom in on an ant mountain in the crack of the curb. He even was fascinated about Teddy's new gold tooth. he decided to crack jokes. "Aye Brah', When we start doing that?"

"Doing what?" Teddy asked as Solo stared into his mouth.

Solo laughed. He had the giggles. He went into a laughing fit and started to point at Teddy as he held his own stomach. Solo had one of them type laughs that made everybody else laugh with him because his sounded so goofy.

Solo was high as he walked. He counted every line on the sidewalk as they neared the court. Teddy and Onyx were mellow and didn't even pay attention to Solo as they walked. Their tolerance for the potent strand of marjuana was way past his.

Shooting the basketball around, they were enjoying a nice sunny day. A few girls were on the side benches with small children and wondering eyes. That made

Solo geek out and take his shirt off in attempt to impress the woman.

A three on three game started shortly when some other players came to get some recreation. It was clean fun. Luckily, they had shorts under their jeans or they would have sweated their outfits out.

Looking outside the gated cage that enclosed the court, a guy was selling bottles of water out of a cooler. Solo was about to go and purchase a few until Onyx intervened. "Hey my man!" The guy tried to ignore him, "Aye Migo!" Onyx jogged up on him, "You cant hear, no habla black man, huh" Onyx asked putting his massive hand on the short guy's shoulder stopping him instantly.

"Sorry, all gone." The guy said, trying to pull the cooler away.

Onyx wasn't going for that. He grabbed the handle out of the guys hand, pulled it back and spinned it around. Opening it, he noticed the guy was lying. He had a frown on his face, then smiled. "Since you say "all gone", imagine these were never here," Onyx said taking three Gatorades out, "you lucky I don't take all this shit." He closed the container and rolled it back to him, "Da Nada, now get the fuck outta' here."

Turning around to face the court he raised the drinks high in the air and yelled, "Yooooo, Ya'll thirty?"

Solo shook his head in shame and looked at Teddy, "That's your mans in nem, that boy a fool."

Looking back in Onyx direction, but past him toward the street, he saw an all black Ducardi motorcycle with a slim woman in a body form fitting biker suit at the light.

The crazy part was the light was green but she didn't make an attempt to pull off. She was sitting idle with both feet on the ground. No one could see her face through the helmet.

'I KNOW SHE GOT TO BE HOT AS SHIT.' Solo thought staring at her.

The biker looked toward the court, lifted her arm balancing the bike between her thighs and began to tap her wrist as if she was asking the time. Solo looked at his watch and it read, 3:00.

"Oh shit!!"

When he looked up to view the cyclist, she did a burn out and rode out on a wheelie. Everybody on the court was in awe at her talent, some looked confused at how the whole scene played out. Solo searched his pocket for the business card. After retrieving it, he noticed a digital message on it. It was weird and had him thinking of the movie "JUMANJI" how the font was wavy and read: YOU LATE.

Onyx made it back to the court and tossed the drink at Solo hitting him in the chest as he tried to hurriedly put his pants on.

"Ayo, you saw Shawty on dat' bike?" Teddy asked looking in the direction of the biker girl then turned to noticed Solo, "Hell you going at?"

Solo looked up hopping on one leg, "I gotta catch a sale." He didn't know why he just lied to his men, but it came so naturally and just felt right at the time. Onyx and Teddy looked at each other with a knowing look. They knew for a fact he lost all his product, but decided against calling him on his bullshit. "Ill be back."

Solo ran down the street as fast as he could. After turning two corners, he was crossing the next intersection when an all black R8 Audi stopped in front of him forcing him to stop. The door made a sound that made Solo back up as the custom butterfly style door opened.

'DAYUM.' Solo thought but held his expression. He leaned over to see who was in the whip.

In a slow seductive tone she spoke. "Konichiwa Utsukushi." It was Yuki. She read his expression and decided to translate her words, "hello, beautiful."

'BEAUTIFUL.' Solo smiled. He put all logic in the back of his mind and fell under her trance. Thoughts of how she just pulled up on him like that never surfaced. All he thought about was that he'd never been called beautiful before.

Yuki pointed to her wrist. "San ji ni, you late."

Solo remembered that meant 3 o' clock from the conversation yesterday. He didn't have a good excuse. Honesty was out of the question. He just rubbed his head. "That was you on the bike? Nah' couldn't had been. I swear it been some weird shit goin' on. But where the hell you come from?" He tried to divert.

Yuki grinned. "Get in." It wasn't a question. Solo shrugged and complied.

In the car, the interior was pink and black. You would have never known looking from the outside in because of its five percent tints. The exterior paint was metallic black with black rims. Yuki looked at him. "You wan' job, right?"

"Hell yeah."

"Put this on." Yuki tossed him a pink bandanna to cover his eyes. Solo looked at her with raised eyebrows; she put a finger to his lips.

"Naisho." She whispered meaning secret as she helped him tied it leaving him blind.

CHAPTER 6

THE MANSION

S olo felt the car stop. It was a smooth ride. Actually, in his mind, it felt like a life sized remote controled car how swift and sharp the turns were. The speed from the take off was incredible, silently he wished he had one for himself. Yuki got out of the car then leaned back in, "Wait."

Solo heard the sound of the hydraulics in the door as it rose up. He didn't move. After five minutes he felt a small, soft but firm hand grab him. Solo stood on his own feel still blindfolded as Yuki whispered directly in his ear with her tongue seductively going in and out.

"You sure you wan' job?"

"Yea! Hell yeah. I need a damn job."

She removed the blindfold.

Solo blinked a few times to get the blur out of his eyes so they could focus on the sight in front of him. Regaining his vision, he looked around. In his sight, he saw five Japanese women in skimpy night attire looking exotic and flirtacious. He looked behind himself and was shocked to see Yuki naked as the day she was born.

"Oh my damn." Solo bit his bottom lip as he looked her up and down. Flawless was the first thought. She called him with a finger. He walked toward her as she backed slowly toward a bed that rotated behind her. She licked her lips.

"So, you think you could handle this job?" Yuki seductively moaned. She knew men thought with their little head not the big one.

Solo continued to walk, oblivious to what the job entails. It didn't matter, if it involved Yuki in this state and other woman, he was all in. Yuki laid down on the bed as the other women crawled in with her. Solo made it closer to the bed and was pushed onto it from behind. Falling on to the mattress, each girl grabbed a limb expertly tying him to the bed post.

Yuki climbed on him and retrieved a chopstick from her head that held her bun together as her hair dropped landing pass her breast. She leaned over so her breast were on Solo's face, he licked them forcing her to giggle.

The chopstick she had was in her hand in clear view as she leaned back up taking the thin covering off it. It was sharp. The dagger was so pointy that you couldn't even see the tip.

"Whoa, whoa!" Solo tried to lean up. He was nervous as he didn't know what Yuki had planned. It sure didn't involve no weapons.

In one quick continuous motion Yuki ran the dagger the length of his body. His clothes fell open like the way a bananas peel would spread. Yuki's beautiful assistants began pulling his clothes off tossing them unto the floor. He was in the nude.

"It's actually alittle chilly in here, aint it?" He asked looking around nervously watching everyone's movements.

Simultaneously the women in the room started licking him from head to toe not missing a spot. His eyes rolled back as the feeling began to feel erotic. One girl got too close to his upper back thigh.

"Time out! Flag on the play!!" He clenched.

She did a quick move with two fingers to the ribs and it made all his muscles relax quickly. Yuki was standing in the nude comfortably in her own skin giving orders as she walked around pointing. Solo couldn't understand a word spoken as she conversed in her native language. After the women licked his whole front side, not missing an area, including his manhood, a mechanical hum was ignited. He paid no attention to the sound, he had high hopes that the sucking would begin, but nope, only licks.

His eyes became bubbled when the bed he was tied to did a crazy maneuver and lowered itself to the floor, leaving him facedown, buttocks up. Now he was scared.

"Please...please don't put nothin' back there." He said a silent prayer.

Starting from his toes the licks continued. Closer and closer they near the glory hole. "OH God...please." He clenched.

Once again, a different lady did a gut punch and he loosened up. "Whoa, wait...oh shit, yup...tongue is in my ass," His facial expression changed, it was a foreign feeling, but it felt good to him, "Don't ya'll tell nobody 'bout this, THEY'LL NEVER BELIEVE YOU!" Solo said tryna look at the culprit.

Yuki laughed. "Humans."

The flipping of the bed process happened again. All the girls walked backward toward the wall where they originally stood. 'WHAT THE FUCK?' Solo thought. It was weird to see them move in sync.

Yuki crawled on the bed and on top of him. His body felt sticky but he put them thoughts to the back of his head as he watched her.

"Damn, I don't know what this is but you sexy as hell." He said looking into her snakelike eyes.

"Can I 'use' your body?" Yuki asked.

"Use? Fuck it, be gentle."

"Yes or no!" She demanded an answer. Confirmation was needed to finish the process as her mouth hovered over his manhood.

"Yes."

She smiled.

Licking the tip, he moaned. Yuki then devoured the length of his tool. Its like she knew her way around as she worked her jaw watching his reactions waiting for the right moment. Solo's eyes rolled back in exstacy. Opening his eyes he noticed Yuki extended her tongue. "Damn." Solo's eyes were big as half dollar coins admiring the length which stretched longer than his manhood.

She tilted her head to the side and wrapped her tongue around his stiffness in the same motion of a snake smothering its prey. He didn't know if it was a new trick or what, he hadn't ever had that done to him before.

She stopped.

Solo made eye contact to see what had happened. Yuki looked at him and kissed the head. "Its time." She winked.

In a few rapid sucks and slurps he became excited all over again as Yuki put her head on his stomach taking him all in. With it in her mouth she inhaled a big breath. In the next breath she took, she sucked so hard that he lifted off the bed making his back arch, then she did the unthinkable... She bit it!

"Ahhhhh!!!" He screamed as he looked down to see there was two fang type teeth deep into his hard on that felt like needles as it pumped some venom-like substance into his shaft.

Yuki released him and his body fell limp. The only feeling solo had was his head. He was paralyzed. He looked down at her with an expression of bewilderment.

"Yuki!? How could you?" Then passed out.

CHAPTER 7

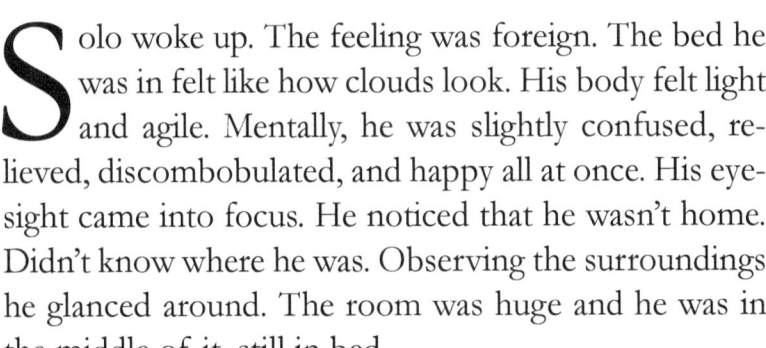

S olo woke up. The feeling was foreign. The bed he was in felt like how clouds look. His body felt light and agile. Mentally, he was slightly confused, relieved, discombobulated, and happy all at once. His eyesight came into focus. He noticed that he wasn't home. Didn't know where he was. Observing the surroundings he glanced around. The room was huge and he was in the middle of it, still in bed.

'WHO PUTS A BED IN THE MIDDLE OF THIS BIG ASS ROOM?' Solo wondered.

Everything besides the bed was aligned against the wall. There were pictures an symbols that lined the wall that were barely visible. That's how big the room was. It could had been a reception area.

Solo squinted his eyes trying to view the wall. In a quick second it was like he was abruptly placed directly in front of the wall, forcing him to fall off the bed thinking he was moving and about to make contact.

Everything magnified. "What...the..fuck?" He blinked, held his eyes closed for a moment then re-opened them. His vision was back to normal. "Oh hell nah!"

His memory started to slowly resurface as he noticed the symbols on the wall were all Japanese kanji. In that instant his eyes bulged, got big as cocaine users as a thought surfaced.

"My dick!!!" He snatched at the sheets to see what was under the material and make sure everything was intact. "Whew!" He was relieved that all was well.

Solo stood up and was naked. He looked around. He could had sworn he'd just had pants on, but it was an illusion. Instead of being sticky, how he remembered being, he was shiny as if he was just dipped in baby oil and smelt great. Looking left, in the corner he saw a jogging suit on the rack. He walked over to it and put the outfit on without any briefs. He thought about checking the dresser just because, but as soon as the idea crossed his mind, the twelve foot double doors opened as he pulled a shirt over his head.

The Japanese chick that entered came in with a straight face, no emotion, but still sexy. Solo grinned. She had on the same exact track suit he had on. She noticed the outfit and smiled. In what seemed like two steps she was in in face with a fist in rotation.

WHOP! WHOP!

Two jabs connected with Solo's face. He tasted blood. "Daijobu?' She asked, smiling.

Surprising Solo, he now understood the language. 'SHE ASKED IF I WAS OKAY.' Solo told himself and smiled. "Hai." He answered, meaning yes.

The attacker threw two more quick jabs than a spinning heel kick to the head. Unlike before, he had an unknown speed and agility. As she threw that vicious combination at him, he watched each strike go past his face and body as he maneuvered out of the way.

She smiled.

She struck again! This time with a jumping double front kick that Solo blocked down as he backed up. He smiled.

Her eyes narrowed and had a slight glow. Irritation was evident.

Solo was nervous. The lady looked crazy. He began to run around the room as she gave chase. He was throwing everything in his path to slow the attacker down as he ran.

"Leave... me.. alone! " He yelled. With each step word a different object flew her way. 'What you want?" Solo asked, stopping at the head of the bed. She was at the foot.

She eyed him and jumped on the bed. Sol thought she was flying as she dived across the bed and tackled him.

"Aww shit, my back." She landed flat on top of him, "Damn you smell good." He inhaled a big breath of her scent.

'SMACK!'

The hit was quick, he couldn't block that one. It surprised him. "Woman...hit me again like that and Ima fu--"

'SMACK!

'kiosukete," (be careful) She warned slowly pulling a shurikin out of nowhere gliding it across his neck.

"Sumimasen!" He apologized, "Don't kill me, You know I was just playing, Ms lady."

Silence.

Out of nowhere, Sol noticed a shadow land behind him with a landing so soft it didn't make a sound. "Arigato." The voice thanked the attacker as she rose to her feet and gave series of bows then backed up and left out.

Still on his back, Solo turned around to see Yuki staring down on him with a smile. "Oh, so you da' Boss 'round here, huh?"

She ignored his questioning with a question of her own, "Daijobu?" She wanted to know if he was okay. Solo officially had it made up in mind that the woman was crazy.

"Nande? (What?) Am I okay? Did you just not see that woman? She was in here tryna' kill me, hell nah' I aint okay," Solo said with wild eyes. "And you, what the hell you do to me? Got me talkin' Japanese, my eyesight funny, and for the record I could have beat her ass but mother raised a gentlemen. She was lucky, I was this close to um umm." Solo said making a sign with his fingers indicating how close he was.

"I gave you gifts." Yuki said

"Gifts? You can have this shit back!"

"You have been chosen for a job. You have accepted. If you neglect your duties, you will be taken care of."

"So you just gonna kill me, huh?" He made a sympathetic face, "Even after our special moment last night. I know you felt something...in here." He pointed and tapped at his heart.

Emotionless she said. "Don't want too but i will, kill you that is."

"Damn, um um, now that's cold-blooded," Accepting his new conditions, he asked, "So what I gotta do?" He began pacing the room to allow the whole day to set in his mind, 'NOBODY NEVER GONNA BELIEVE THIS SHIT, SHE HAD FANGS LAST NIGHT, NOW SHE GOT A KODAK SMILE. I GOTS TO BE TRIPPIN'. I GOTTA BE DREAMIN' Sole thought inside his head.

"No, you're not dreaming." Yuki said.

Solo looked back at here across the room, "Did I say that out loud?"

She smiled.

Turning back around , she appeared behind him. Alittle startled, he jumped. He could had sworn she was just across the way, but there she was. "Listen," Yuki began." Ill give you a day to process this. It'll also give you time to adjust and practice your new abilities. Embrace them and you'll master them. Tell your mother you finally got that new job. You're a driver now,ummm, for a Diplomat of Japan."

When Yuki mentioned his mother, it pulled a string. His assumption was it was a threat. he became defensive. "What you say 'bout my mama?' Solo asked as he tried to sneak a haymaker punch toward Yuki.

The new strength and speed he now possessed made the punch come super fast making him fall face first as Yuki side stepped then and laughed.

"Look at you, just leave. Practice and Ill see you tomorrow, sayonara." She said waving as she turned on her heels.

"Chotto Matte!!" Solo called behind her telling her to (hold on),"Doki ni?" (Where?)

"Koki ni." (Right here) She responded then put a finger to her lips, "Naisho." She said meaning (secret) as she narrowed her eyes as a silent threat.

"Wakarmashta." He replied. (Understood)

"Ja mata," (see you later) She smiled, "One of the seekers will help you from here."

"Seekers?" He questioned.

"you'll see." With that she was gone.

CHAPTER 8

Solo sat in the room thinking, really just trying to take into account the last 24 hours of his of life as he gathered his thoughts. Standing up, he started to shadow box and figure out what "gifts" he now possessed. Running full speed to the end of the room, instinctively he ran up the wall into a back flip.

"Ooooooh Shit!" Solo sang in amazement still in the air as his body rotated. It felt like he was flipping in slow motion. When he landed, he took a bow to the imaginary audience.

'FATE SEEKER, HUH?' Solo pondered on the thought.

Really all he wanted to know was what it all meant. Why did Yuki want him to tell his mother that he was a driver? In his opinion, a driver didn't need these type of abilities that he now had. Gifts, as he was told. Thinking back on how he received them, he shivered. "Um, never again."

Solo felt good, light on his toes as if he could do anything. Still, he wondered what other gifts he had, what were the side effects and or defects. Question rushed his head, a thousand thoughts a minute. Looking around the room, it was quiet. He was wondering if he could just up and leave or if he needed to wait or even ask.

Still, Solo didn't know where he was at. He remembered being blindfolded then everything was a blur. Walking toward the door, the double doors, he pushed them in an attempt get through.

"These joints heavy as shit." Solo said straining as he pushed.

No luck.

He took a few steps back trying to gain momentum and more 'umph' he pushed again. As fast as it opened it swung back faster knocking him ten feet back.

"Ahh Shit," He said jumping up back up, "My ass!" He rubbed it in quick motions for comfort.

He then knew strength was a gift. Headed for the door again, this time he took a deep breath to try and channel his energy and pushed. It still felt super heavy but with his new mental, it opened easily.

Entering the hallway, the same girl that was trying to beat him up appeared before him. He looked her up and down. "What? You must be some type of side kick or some shit. Yuki gone. She cant save you now."

She smiled ignoring his comments. "Ohayou Gazaimas." She said said with a sneaky smile as if she just met him and wasn't there a few minutes ago with a knife to his throat.

Solo looked at her. "Good morning to you too." He responded as he tried to walk past but to no avail. She cut in front of him.

"Chotto Matte," She said placing her hand on his chest.

"Hold on for what?" He smacked her hand down.

With a finger she pointed. "Hidari," She gave him directions to move "left". He complied and walked to the room as directed and opened the door.

The whole room was a big walk-in closet. A smile naturally came across his face. Solo looked back at her with questioning eyes, now hiding his smile. Inside was brand new everything. Clothes and accessories.

"Erabeto." She smiled.

"Choose what?"

She pointed to the closet and pushed him further into the room. "For me?" Solo pointed to himself, he needed the confirmation like he had heard once before.

"Hai."

"You sure."

"Hai, yakusoku." She promised.

"That cool, I need some new threads, Arigato," Solo said thanking her with his hands together taking a bow.

He turned around and whispered, "Witcho' ugly ass." Then pulled a shirt off the rack.

In half a second he felt the pain of a foot kicking him forward into the very same rack he grabbed the shirt.

"Damn woman! what you do that for?" Solo asked rubbing his back.

In broken English she replied. I understand, you ugly." then walked out.

Solo stood up and fixed himself. "Keep putting your hands on me, Ima whoop dat as." He mumbled.

Looking through the different brands of clothes, Solo didn't know what to grab or even how many he was allowed to get. Him being in there too long undecided the lady peeked in telling him to choose one and hurry.

He figured they were replacing the clothes that were destroyed the night before. Knowing this, he settled on Hugo Boss button up and some cool jeans. There was even a glasses rack, from there he spotted a pair of Ray bands and made them a part of his outfit. For his shoe wear, he grabbed a pair of Silver Dunkin's (Tim Duncan).

He was surprised a group of Asian women would even have them type of shoes. "I look sweet." Solo admired himself leaving out of the room. The angry lady was right there looking frustrated. "Whets your name anyway?"

She looked at him and began walking away but still answered, "Sarang."

"Love," He repeated her name translated. "Utsukushi namae." He replied informing her that her name was beautiful.

Sarang paused for a second. Solo could see her smile from behind her. Sarang continued to walk. All women around the world love a compliment, even if this particular woman was a killing machine.

Strolling through the hallway, it was long. Solo started to realize that he was in a mansion. The domain was laid out. Nice would be an understatement. Chandeliers were everywhere high in the ceiling, expensive artwork in thick wooden frames that could mistakenly be assumed they cost more than the actual artwork. Statues appeared to be years old, antique quality. He felt like it was the Museum of Modern Art he was walking through.

Passing the multiple rooms, he noticed different women. All the rooms were door less. Some women were relaxing, some naked, or just in leisure clothes. When he paused to get a better look they wouldn't cover up or even look shocked. All of them would speak saying, "Konichiwa Otason."

Solo looked at Sarang. "Why they all keep calling me, Father?"

Sarang looked at him, "That who you are now, courtesy of Yuki but I wont be calling you that, capeesh."

He smiled. Solo didn't know what that meant, or entailed, but it sounded good coming off their lips every time.

They walked what seemed like twenty minutes to finally make it to a garage in front of what looked more like an estate to him now. Sarang pressed the garage door opener and six doors opened simultaneously.

His jaws dropped.

"Erabeto." Sarang told him to choose.

All exotic and luxury cars were before him. Thinking of his neighborhood he knew he couldn't just pull up in nothing too crazy without raising eyebrows or questions being asked. There was a Rolls Royce, Maserati,Lambo', Audi, Beamer's and Benzes'. He looked past all them when he noticed a pretty royal blue and black Ducarti. "Hey baby!" He eyed the bike.

Solo loved bikes and knew him pulling upon that wouldn't attract suspicion.

Sarang told him that the keys were already inside the ignition and the bike was his to take, along with all the other vehicles in the garage. They were at his personal disposal when needed. Every vehicle was registered and insured with Diplomatic Immunity.

After getting on the bike and starting it up, he was all smiles. Sarang walked up on Solo giving him a brand new I-phone.

"Take! Answer always phone." he accepted the phone and kicked the bike down a gear putting it into first when she grabbed his shoulder.

"Naisho," She reminded him to keep everything a secret.

CHAPTER 9

UPTOWN, WASHINGTON D.C.

Solo was cruising the city streets on his new bike. The weather was perfect to ride. No heavy winds, only slight breezes with clear skies. The sun was lightening the sky at a moderate temperature. He was enjoying all the stares and glances that came his way from both female and male viewers. It seemed like the world could tell when someone was on a come up.

Solo didn't go straight home. His stomach was doing back flips and he decided to stop at a diner. Brunch was still being served. He never understood brunch, it made no sense to him. All you did was wait in line for an hour to essentially get lunch. He shook the thought as his phone vibrated:

'AMERICAN EXPRESS CARD
IN BACK COMPARTMENT
UNDER SEAT, YOURS'

He smiled.

Solo stood in front of the diner that was named 'STEAK -N- EGGS'. To most, it was a night spot. That when the most revenue would roll in. The after the club crowd kept the restaurant open even though it was a 24 hour location.

This time of the day usually drew in the neighborhood customers. Walking into the establishment he ordered steak, eggs, and waffles. He was about to step off but thought of his mother and little brother. He had a new visa so he figured why not treat?

"Aye' my man, my bad. Can I add to the order?"

"You sure can!" The cashier responded with a smile knowing more money was going to be exchanged.

"Bet! But I need this order to go..." Solo informed him and paused to think, "...Uhh, let me get uh, like six pancakes, four fried eggs with cheese and uh, make sure they fry the eggs hard and turkey bacon and some sausage links."

"No problem, that'll be $45.00."

The cashier smiled.

"Damn, you add that up right?" Solo asked giving him the fresh platinum card.

The cashier, chef didn't even respond. All he did was slide the receipt and pointed to the dotted line.

"Sign here." He said with a stern face.

"Damn, what happened to the nice guy, "Solo shook his head. "And we suppose to be brothers." He said after signing and placing the pen on the counter.

Next door to the diner was a convenience store. Solo entered. Going straight to the counter he asked for a pack of cigarettes. As he was about to give the clerk his card, a guy ran in the store with a sawed off shotgun pointed. Solo raised his hands high to the sky.

"Shit! this that bullshit, I cant get a break."

Running directly tot the counter beside Solo, the robber placed the barrel of the gun to the clerk's face as he tossed a bag at his chest, "Fill it up, Apu!"

The clerk complied quickly emptying the contents of the register. A few seconds later the bag was full of cash. Solo stood frozen, not trying to provoke the villain. He knew he wasn't no hero. The double doors in the back of the store flew open and the owner came from the other side.

"Oh hell nah!!"

BOOM!

The store owner shot the newspaper stand that was in between Solo and the robber making it rain papers. They both flinched. "Mother lover tryna rob me!!!" The owner yelled as he began reloading his one shot rifle dropping the used shell on the ground.

Solo's reflexes came to life as the robber was turning his gun on the owner, ready to squeeze. In a swift, calculated jab to the shooters forearm, a bone and its tendons shattered on impact. As the jab followed through, with his right hand, Solo grabbed the lottery ticket scanner, pulling the wires, bolts and all, then threw it at the store owner as he chambered the bullet.

It connected with his head forcing the owner to fall back as a shot was released to the ceiling. It was a precautionary measure, the store owner seemed to have an itchy trigger finger and Solo didn't want to become a wrongfully accused statistic.

Solo turned his attention back to the would be robber, who was yelling in agony holding his arm. His weapon now on the floor. Solo threw a straight jab to the chest, the robber flew ten feet into a rack that held a variety of chips. Solo picked the gun up and looked at the cashier, who was frozen in place with his hands still up.

"Put cho' hands down, Fool!" Solo said.

Shaky and scared, he complied. Solo walked closer and handed him the gun, and nodded, "Watch him." He motioned to the semi- conscience robber. "Call the police, but before you do, give me my pack of cigarettes and you pay for 'em."

CHAPTER 10

BACK AT THE MANSION

"When do you need this done?" Sarang asked, anxious to make Yuki proud.

"Yesterday," Yuki replied with clenched teeth. "Fate has spoken and fate will be done."

Sarang was the best, next to Yuki. The mission was given and she was ready. Inside she felt a little mad that Yuki felt she needed to bring on Solo. She knew if she would had sent her to do the Ethan job, it would had been completed. She vowed to herself from this day forth she would always complete the mission no matter what in order to stay in the good graces of her leader, Yuki.

She left the estate with her itinerary of the mark. Shawn 'chopper' Williams. He was a gang banger that resided in a neighborhood that mostly housed lower class Blacks and Latinos. The complex was huge. If you weren't a resident in the area you would stick out like a sore thumb.

Sarang had an address. She was camped outside of the complex, a few buildings down. this was safer. For them. There were about fifteen or so guys on the top stoop mingling around going here and there. She could had walked up to his apartment, but her foreign descent would had brought too much attention and could've violated their creed of action as Fate Seekers.

In the car she sat, she waited.

It was Friday, unknown to Sarang, in the projects all around the country it was the night to chill and take a load off. Some people would enjoy a night at the club, others hugged the block and chilled. still it was early. The sun was orange, still glowing but making its descent.

'PATIENCE' Sarang thought to herself as she sat in her all black Mercedes.

People walked by, some admired the car, others plotted, thinking of some kind of way to come up. Sarang could see the thirst in their eyes, they couldn't see her behind the limo' style tints. No one seemed to notice that she pulled up and never exited the vehicle.

After about two hours of sitting idle in the parking lot Sarang spotted her mark. Choppa. He seemed to be the man in his area. Everyone he past put a hand out in attempts to get recognition.

"I'm ;bout to ride to get some mo' drinks." Choppa told a guy.

"Ite, Big Homie, but you know the liquor store closed on the corner, right?"

"Yeah I'm hip'. I'm 'bout to head to da' one on The Pike."

"Oh the bootleg joint, that a bet. Need me to roll wit' you?"

Choppa giggled. "Nah, Bruh, don't need you on the back of my bike." He said putting his biker gloves.

Choppa got on his motorcycle and be gan zipping up his North face jacket in an attempt to conceal his Mac-11 sub machine gun under his armpit with a shoestring for support as if it was a purse. Once it was secured he started his bike and pulled off.

Sarang watched as Choppa cruised past. Pulling out of the lot, she began to tail hi. She was a secure ten car length behind. With her vision, she might as well been on his muffler. Choppa was eastbound riding down Pennsylvania Avenue heading to the beltway.

'NOT SMART, MR. CHOPPA' Sarang smiled.

Merging onto the highway, Choppa opened up the throttle and the bike took off. Luckily for Sarang, she was in a Mercedes CL Coupe or he would had been gone with the wind. She sped up switching lanes as she neared. Catching up to the motorcycle, side by side they sped.

Sarang lowered her window, Choppa looked to his right noticing her. Upon recognition of a female driver he smile letting his guard down. "What's up Shawty?" He asked with a head nod.

Sarang smiled then responded. "Fate." She pulled out a black and chrome .40 caliber Glock and fired at the gas tank. Not knowing the bike was custom made, the bullets didn't inflict any damage. The bike was metal plated in all the necessary areas.

Choppa immediately slowed hid bike with the back brakes, slightly skidding the back tire to regain control. Sarang slowed also. Coming up beside Choppa she was shocked to notice him brandishing an all black Mac-11. With wide eyes she took cover.

A fire holes of bullets left the machine gun as she stomped the gas making the car swerve unto the off ramp as the windows shattered. Choppa put his bike into gear and gunned it, trying to make his escape. The bike was fast, but not fast enough. Sarang gained control and gave chase. Choppa looked back and saw her gaining. He reached back with gun in hand and fired. The gun sent multiple rounds then began to 'click'.

"Shit!" He was out of ammo

Pulling close behind Choppa, Sarang rammed him from behind. Choppa swerved but maintained control. In and out of traffic the chase continued. Sarang fired her weapon, she only fired at the bike. It had to appear as an accident, not a homicide.

Sarang drove beside him and saw an opening. She rammed him again. Choppa looked over to her, "Fuck is you doing? You crazy Bitch!"

Sarang ignored him a she pulled to the right of the bike. With a strong bump, Choppa was forced to the median of the road which was grass that separated the on coming traffic on the opposite side. Choppa lost control. All Sarang heard was multiple tires screeching, then a few car horns blare as the bike went into oncoming traffic. Most of the cars managed to swerve out of the way of Choppa all except an eighteen wheeler carry flammable contents.

The loud explosion along with the high pitch sounds of scraping metal and steel confirmed her job, mission complete.

Sarang drove in silence leaving her with only thoughts. Disappointment etched her face as she gripped the steering wheel heading back to the mansion. She underestimated the gang banger and the result was almost her life.

'YUKI IS GOING TO BE FURIOUS' She thought as she finally noticed the damage that was done to the vehicle. It was in terrible condition, to make matters worse, each mission was to be a clean kill, no mistakes or traces of their existence left behind.

The car itself was a tell-tell sign that the mission wasn't clean. Crazy enough, Sarang had to drive the car all the way back in that condition with hopes of nobody pointing he vehicle out or paying too close attention. the only thing on her side was the time. It was 2:00am and the streets were empty.

Pulling up to the mansion, Sarang slid her card down the key access panel gaining entry to the gated state. Coming through the long driveway, Yuki stood at the top of the stairs in a night robe looking down as Sarang came to a stop.

With her head low, Sarang exited the car. "Yuki--" She began but was silenced with a hand.

"Who?"

Sarang raised her head, "Sumimasen," She apologized. "Okason,"She called her mother. "The job is complete but it got a little messy." She spoke in a whisper.

"Diajobu?' She asked if she was okay.

"Hai. I'm fine."

Yuki looked her over, "And you wonder why I said we needed a new look."

The one statement was worse than any punishment she could have received. It was an insult on her skills.

"Move it!" Yuki demanded.

"Nande!?" She was confused and asked what?

"Kuruma." Yuki pointed to the car.

"Hai, Okason." Yes mother she replied, getting back in the car ready to move the damaged vehicle that was releasing black smoke.

CHAPTER 11

EARLIER THAT DAY...

Solo walked through the parking lot after he parked his new bike. he could feel the stares as he walked through the complex.

"Glad I didn't get that, Lambo', shit." He said to himself.

Opening his door, he was met by his mother, "Where was your antennas last night? You know I needed you to bring that a/c unit up them stairs."

"My bad, Ma. But guess what" Solo was excited to give his mother the news.

"What's in the bag? Valerie redirected, "Is that some food?"

"yea, Ma, it's for you for you and Riley."

"Good! cause I'm hungry and sure don't feel like turning that stove on," She said grabbing the bag, "Riley! Come down here and eat, child!"

Solo blew a sigh as he shook his head. His mother was ignoring what he was trying to sat. Riley came running down the stairs two at a time then noticed Solo and slowed down. Riley remembered what he did to his big brother yesterday and knew payback was inevitable.

Valerie headed to the kitchen, Solo stood in front of his little brother with a grin on his face. "Well well well, I told you Ill get you back, Punk."Solo said rubbing his hands together.

"Solo!!" Valerie called from the kitchen oblivious to what was going on around the corner. That was all Riley needed. In that quick second, he jumped over the rail like it was a fence and did a beeline to the table and jumped in a chair. Solo was surprised at Riley's efforts.

"Sneaky lil' bastard."

Going into the kitchen, Solo leaned against the counter near the sink, "Ma, I'm trying to talk to you and tell you something."

"What is it, Boy?" She said stopping what she was doing giving him the attention he was seeking.

"I, gots, me, a jizob'." He said in his best Mike Epps voice as he smiled proud to please his mother.

With opened arms she rushed him giving him a kiss, "What kind of job is it?"

Thinking of the job title Yuki gave him, he responded "I'm a driver...for a Japanese Diplomat."

"Diplomat! How in heavens name did you get a job like that?" She was shocked. You can barely drive yourself. It sounds like it could be dangerous. You don't know what them people got going on over there."

That last comment made Solo pause and think. It was like a mother's intuition to always know what's up with their child in a sense but not 100%. "Cat got your tongue, Boy? I asked you a question?"

"Nah' Ma, it was a hook up, well somebody pulled some strings for me. Plus they gave me an estate bike for my own transportation when I'm off. How cool is that? She's nice."

"Oh it's a she," Valerie said with a knowing smile. "You better keep business and pleasure separate."

"I know, Ma."

Today the neighborhood, well projects, because it sure didn't have the Mr. Roger's feel to it, was busy. It was Friday. Turn up was almost guaranteed. Everybody was hustling up some money just to blow it that night. Solo was headed to Ebony's house. He had intentions on seeing her last night but the episode with Yuki prevented him from getting back up with her. Solo knew she was probably livid.

Making it to her door, he knocked. His ear was to the door and he heard the TV on and knew someone was home. But then again, Solo realized he does the same thing sometime; leave the TV on to give the illusion that someone is home to possibly scare away home invaders.

Turning to leave, the door opened."What you want?" Ebony's mother answered the door. She didn't really care for Solo. His name was well known in the neighborhood and it wasn't in a good light.

"How you doing, Ms Reynolds, Is Ebony here?"

"Nope! She out doing some last minute shopping so she could leave and get her education, something alot of you hoodlums should be doing around here." She said then slammed the door in his face.

Solo stomped the ground and it cracked. He had a tight face and clenched jaw. He had to contain his temper. He wanted to curse her out but took a few breaths as he turned to leave.

Leaving the porch, Teddy came around the corner. Solo didn't notice him as he was fuming and walking in the opposite direction, mumbling to himself.

Walking nowhere in particular, Onyx was approaching him. With an extended hand, Solo was in the process of greeting Onyx when Teddy came from behind him putting soli in a chicken wing hold.

Solo's body tensed and swelled up.

Instinct kicked in.

Beings though his elbows were spread wide, instead of closing them in attempt to overpower his assailant, his arms went backward, the way flexible or double jointed people were able to do with ease.

Only difference was it wasn't done slowly. It was quick and connected with Teddy's head making him instantly release his hold. Free from Teddy's grasp, Solo swatted, did a spinning clip move, sweeping Teddy's feet from underneath him. Teddy landed on his back as Solo jumped on top to finish him off.

"Solo!!" Onyx yelled, snapping him out his trance. "What da' hell you doing. Strong man." He said rushing to help Teddy up.

"Oh shit! My bad. What hell you sneaking up on me for anyway? You know i be lunchin'." (meaning tripping)

Rubbing his head getting up slowly Teddy said, "I should whoop your ass," He looked at his now dirty white tee, "Where you learn that shit from anyway?"

"It was a reflex. I just did it, my bad."

They began to walk off, Solo tried to change the course of conversation but failed. More questions followed.

"Where you go yesterday? Teddy asked, before Solo could give an answer Onyx followed up with another question of his own. "Where dat' bike come from, it look sweet. And that joint got Dip' tags."

Solo began, "When I was going to catch that sale, right..."

Teddy and Onyx looked at each other as if they knew Solo was about to come up with an extravagant story out of nowhere.

"...Nah' for real," he continued. "I was gonna catch a sale but dude who I was about to serve had other plans. You know I been servin' him since like junior high school, right?" Solo paused to see if they would comment, but they didn't, "...so he asked if I had a clear driving record and offered me a job."

"So you mean to tell me a crack head is a Diplomat? Teddy asked with a suspicious expression like he heard it all now.

"No man! But the employer is a Diplomat and she gave me the bike 'cause she live waaaayy uptown. All I gotta do is ride her around when she calls. Sweet money and I started last night."

They shook their heads like whatever, and continued to walk. "At least you got a gig' now," Onyx said. "Matter fact let me get a loan Mr. Sweet money."

Damn, Cuz! I aint get paid yet. It aint no pay as you go. Matter fact, I don't even know what I'm getting paid, yet."

With that being said Solo's phone vibrated. It was a text:

'2100 M STREET N.W

GET THERE NOW'

"you got a phone too!" Teddy acknowledged.

"Business only, and speaking on that, I gotta go. Solo said flashing them the message.

CHAPTER 12

THE DOJO

S olo didn't have the slightest idea what the text meant, he just knew it only said 'NOW'. From the past experiences with Yuki, he knew she didn't play. And he didn't want to get fired on his first assignment on his first official day. Even though the occupation was still fully not understood he was gamed. All he did understand was the fact that he was chosen.

The address on the text was a place Sol had never been. On his Google maps app it appeared and was located uptown.

The Georgetown area.

This was an area for the rich and wealthy. It was common for people like Solo to get lost or be out of the loop in this area. Too many streets streets were private like. Cruising down a side street that appeared as if there weren't any sidewalks, the cars parked dangerously close to each other and the row homes. If you opened your door too wide, it might just hit the front entrance. To add to the conjunction, it was a two way traffic.

The map had him lost, a lot of the side streets weren't listed that he was passing. After riding and asking a few people for directions that would talk to him, he made it to the address. It was carved in stone stretched across an old looking building.

Architects and brick masons would quickly notice the integrity of the building. It was ancient and had the type of bricks that weren't even in development anymore. The kind that could withstand any storm and stand tall. The spot had history.

Walking up the steps, Solo stood at the door and was about to knock but didn't. Only reason being, as he reached to make contact it opened slowly by itself.

He leaned in with his head first. The area in front of him was pitch black. There was a hanging lamp light that only lit a circle on the floor in the middle of what he assumed was a narrow hallway. Solo couldn't see a thing.

"Hello..." It was an eerie silence. Solo took a few steps forward, entering. "Yo! Anybody here, I was told to come here by Yuki, it seemed urgent." Solo said looking around trying to zoom in on anything.

"Konichiwa." A voice said from behind Solo.

"What the fu-?" Solo spun around quickly, "How you get behind me like that?"

When Solo turned around, there wasn't anyone present, only a presence but not visible. He could feel he wasn't in the area alone. He was slightly nervous. It quickly disappeared when he remembered he wasn't the average person any more.

A boost of confidence came over him, "Show yourself so I could beat your ass!"

"Gambette." The voice said wishing him good luck.

Starting from the entrance and ending at the back wall, lights began to flick on by the section until the whole area was bright. The area Solo thought was a hallway was actually the complete opposite.

He was in a dojo.

Between fifteen to twenty young students sat on their knees along the wall silently observing him. Solo was surprised, maybe even shocked but he'd never admit it. The ages ranged from children to adolescents. A teacher had to be close. Solo scanned the area but couldn't see anyone fitting the description. He stood still, waiting for someone to make a move.

"Sora!" A student said pointing up. Solo knew that the word meant sky, his natural instinct was to look up. Looking toward the ceiling a man was coming from the air.

The ceiling slightly stole his attention. It resembled the actual sky, literally. There was a painting so precise and accurate you would believe there wasn't a roof. The guy landed really soft, like he took a step, not as if he just landed from no telling how many feet in the air.

"Mise?" He asked.

"Student? Nah' I aint one of them." Solo said nodding toward the students along the wall.

"Hai, you are."

"Oh really, do it look like I'm in school?"

The man smiled. He had on an oversized robe with his hands together covered by the lengthiness of the sleeves. The students looked on in awe. They could feel the tension rising. Many were excited to see the man teach the new comer a lesson, but the teacher held his composure.

"Well, not school but training." The man replied.

"Training for what?"

"Your job. I'm the sensei."

"Well lets go then." Solo said bouncing up an down on his toes, moving his neck side to side, feeling himself, then rushed the Sensei.

Solo threw a left! Sensei blocked it by smacking his hand down the way a parent does when telling a child not to touch. Solo threw a right hook! Sensei grabbed his fist right before it connected stopping it on his own cheek.

Squeezing Solo's hand, his knuckles cracked. "Ahhh!" He screamed coming down on a knee. Solo punched him in his gut with the left.

Sensei smiled. No effect.

That only infuriated Solo as he screamed. Sensei still held unto his right hand tightly. This time Solo threw the same left as Sensei was talking to the students making a point never paying attention to Solo.

His gift.

It was in full effect, his eyes turned snake-like wild, and the punch came with extreme power and force. When it connected, it forced Sensei off his feet and soaring in to the air.

Sensei landed hard. Solo ran in a half second, what would had taken the average man much more strides, and was on top of him about to continue the assault until, "Chotta Matte!" Sensei called out, telling him to hold on. Solo looked at him, his nerves began to calm, his heart rate sowed and he composed himself.

"Sumimasen." Solo apologized extending a hand out to help pick up the teacher.

"This is why you are here," Sensei smiled. "To learn control and how to channel all you r gifts on demand."

"Oh okay, so where do we begin?"

"Koki ni." Meaning right here.

CHAPTER 13

BACK AT THE MANSION

Yuki walked back into the mansion. It seemed as if fate was working overtime. She had all the fate seekers out in differnt areas of the world. There was still another mission that needed to be taken care of for this cycle of fates to be completed. Yuki was sitting in one of the many leisure rooms, sipping hot green tea that the server brought her. She was still upset with Sarang for m,making such a mess the other night, especially to the car. It hurt Yuki to her soul to have it done, but she had to have the car destroyed.

The accident was all over the news, a few motorist gave a description of the Benz Sarang drove claiming different scenarios of the highway shoot out. Multiple bullet casings were recovered. When it came to cars, Yuki loved the man made machines, she cherished each one she owned. Never would you find dirt or any defects on them. The thought of her Benz made her mad all over again.

Sarang came into the house, she wasn't scared but was nervous as she searched for Yuki. The mansion was massive. Finding people could be a task in itself. Room after room she passed and came up empty. Every room seemed to be unoccupied, then she came up on the only door in the estate that had an all black door with a red dot. As she neared the door to open it, a lightbulb above her blew out along with the rest down the hallway leaving it pitch black.

One by one they lit back up and stopped in front of one room and flickered. Giving the all black door one final look, Sarang turned away and headed to the room where the light flickered.

Opening the door, Yuki was on the other side sitting on a sofa with a black cat on her lap glaring at Sarang. Sarang knew she messed up and was in for type of displinary action.

"Okason." Sarang acknowledged with a bow.

Yuki nodded, "Sit."

Sarang came into the presence of Yuki and sat on her knees with both hands placed flat on her thighs. Yuki looked at her as she rubbed the cat then spoke in a low tone.

"I don't know what's gotten into you but it's not of your character to be so messy. I sent you to destroy the car, "She paused and exhaled a sigh. "because you made our presence known. We are only inhabitants on this planet for one reason, and that's to carry out fates obligations, silently. But you, you want to march to the bet of your own drum, "Yuki stood up and the cat jumped off her ;lap and ran off as she paced, "So I have a special mission for you. I was going to wait and give you help but I changed my mind. If you die, back to the seventh Dimension you will be condemned. That will be a lesson learned,

"If you live, same result, lesson learned. Anyhow I win and you WILL think twice before you start making your own rules and disobeying mines. No matter how easy you think a mission is, quietly and discreet is key. No trace of your arrival or departure. Here." Yuki tossed an itinerary at Sarang.

Sarang looked at her mission sheet and instantly lowered her head. The mission, her mission, was an Italian Mob Boss. the guy was always surrounded by goons with heavy arsenal. Looking up from the missions information, she pleaded, "Please, Okasan, let me get help. I need more hands."

"Maybe you do, but I wouldn't..." Yuki said matter factly. "...since you move as if you're the head of the snake apparently and do things your way, complete this however you please. Ill be sending you in a couple days."

Yuki said, shooing Sarang away as Solo came through the door.

Yuki turned to attention to him, "Did you meet with the Sensei?"

Solo looked at Sarang and gave her a head nod, "Sup' Boo, you miss me?" Sarang stood and bowed to Yuki and turned to leave, ignoring Solo, "Sup' wit' her, Whoa!" The black cat ran into the room passing Sol and jumped in Yuki's arms. "but yeah, I met him earlier, cool guy or whatever,he taught me a lot," Solo said sitting on the nearest couch. "You called me here, so here I am."

Yuki smiled at him. "What did you learn, matter fact show me." She said jumping up from the seat, gliding at Solo kicking him out the couch onto the floor.

He stood up. He smiled as his eyes turned snake-like which heightened his senses and abilities. Yuki grinned, placing the cat on the ground.

"Oh, you're learning control." She said as she squinted her eyes and did the same. Running to each other the sparing session began.

Sarang was in her room. She was livid, but understood. Yuki was all business and she had to understand it was a priveledge to be on this planet. Sarang trained her whole life for this opportunity and she planned on taking over as the head of the snake.

The estate had been around for many years and it hadn't survived this long from it's seekers being sloppy. never leave a trace of evidence linked to your job, unless everybody that saw something was dead. that was instilled in all of the seekers as the Sensei trained each and everyone of them.

Sarang began packing her bags. New York was the destination on the itinerary. Tiny Ramos. The leader of an organized crime syndicate in the Big Apple. The mission of killing him wouldn't be easy, in essence. The killing part would be easy, but without weapons for herself made it a little difficult when the whole security detail had plenty of guns.

With her bag in tow, Sarang passes Yuki in a room with Solo in there fighting each other like enemies. "He's pretty good." Sarang thought passing them by heading for the airport.

At the ground level,Sarang was stopped by the black cat as it paused in front of her. "What you want?" The cat looked at her, then to the door. Sarang opened the door and the cat ran through the door, leaping, instantly turning into an eagle and flying away.

The eagle was Yuki's pet from The Otherworld. It had the power to change into anything Yuki wanted and needed it to be. Right now, it was off to soar the skies and check on the other seekers, a secret spy only Sarang knew about. Sarang pretty much knew everything that Yuki did; hence the reason why she was always on Sarang's case about any and everything. Yuki takes her position seriously, and any failures would result in being cast back to the Fate lands to be punished, severely.

Making it to the airport, getting through security was fast and hassle free. With the diplomatic credentials the staff didn't want any problems with bosses so it was swift.

First class. Sarang wouldn't have it any other way. Sitting back in the plush seats, she sipped wine, then eventually closed her eyes as the plane began to ascend into the skies.

Solo tasted blood as he glared at Yuki from one knee. The bitter taste only excited him more. Yuki was unfazed. He was relentless and determined, Solo rushed her again with a three jab combination in attempts to connect with Yuki's face. All his swings were weaved except the last hook, it connected with her chi.

Shocked at the connection, Yuki responded with a spinning hay- maker with her fist clenched together as her arm extending through Solo's stomach sending his body in the air. It was powerful. Solo felt her fist touch his spine as he flew across the room through the wall into the next room,

"Ahh, my stomach." Solo groaned getting up holding his midsection. Yuki jumped through the hole in the wall landing directly in front of Solo.

"Daijobu?" Yuki asked.

Solo looked up at her and shook his head. "Hell nah', I'm not okay! You cheated! What you hit me with?"

"Good training. Get yourself in shower, be out front in fifteen minutes, Driver." Yuki said, dropping her clothes in a trail as she headed for the shower.

"Can I come with you? We could help each other out, y'know, you wash my back, I wash yours," Solo said trying to walk, then fell back to a knee. "Ahh,maybe next time, rain check."

As if it was clockwork, a server came in the room with a wheel chair. She helped Solo to the shower. He became confused when the lady pulled a chopstick out her bun. Pulling the thin cover off, it exposed a knife.

Damn, what all the people here carry some type of weapons?" He asked, shocked.

She smiled. "Hai."

In the same motion and precision, the maid sliced through Solo's shirt. "I could have just taken it off." She picked him up like a child, then cut through his pants without ever dropping him. He was now naked, hanging from her shoulders as she laid him in the shower in a fetal position.

The shower was huge, she turned on the water. Solo tried to stand but his body felt paralyzed. "Wait!" The maid told him, "Water special, make you feel better." She then pushed him further and let the water hit him.

Within seconds, Solo began to get feeling in his body. He smiled. "I'm back, Baby!" He stood up reaching for the soap. The water was white and thick, as soon as he grabbed a wash rag the water turned clear and regular. The maid returned to the door and grabbed the wheel chair.

"Five minutes, Yuki waits." She said leaving,never looking back.

Rushing his shower, Solo did a quick wash then turned the water off. Leaving the shower, there was an all black Armani suit on a mannequin. He assumed it was his because once again he was cut out of his clothes.

Putting the attire on, he jogged through the mansion to the awaiting car. Yuki stood at the back door, Solo looked at her and she nodded toward the door.

"Oh snap, my bad," Solo reached for the handle to let her in. "After you Ma'am."

Inspecting the car, Solo walked around to the driver seat. It was a Bentley Continental. 'I KNOW THIS JOINT COST THAT BAG!' Solo thought as he admired the car. A maid at the bottom of the stairs held a platter with the key in the center of it. Solo grabbed them off and sat in the car.

Damn, it smell sexy in here." He said to himself.

Yuki lowered the divider that separated them and spoke, "Go to this location." She said interrupting his thoughts.

"Yup, got it, Boss." Solo said, sarcasm in his voice. Yuki didn't laugh, but she responded.

"See how funny you are in a few minutes." She raised the divider back up.

Solo didn't really pay the comment any attention. He noticed a USB connection input and decided to plug his phone into it. He put the address in the navigational system and was on his way.

CHAPTER 14

NEW YORK CITY

L anding in the Big Apple, Sarang was ready and fully aware of the mission that was ahead of her. She was to be an exported escort from across the waters, someone different and foreign was what he requested. His original "package" was intercepted and here arrived the replacement.

Sarang.

The airport was busy, she walked sown the terminal and noticed the different signs from the families awaiting their loved ones. Sarang spotted her sign: FOREIGN GOODESS

A big stocky Italian was holding the sign across his chest just standing there. He wasn't making any attempts to search and notice her. Sarang came up on the guy, "Hai!" She faked a smile and point to the sign.

"You don't speak English?"

Sarang played stupid as far as the language only responding with the name she had on her hit lit. "Tony?"

The Italian grabbed Sarang by her arm escorting her out the airport. Out front was a limo; the driver opened the door. He grabbed Sarang's carry on bag politely and placed it in the trunk.

Entering the back of the luxurious vehicle, Sarang noticed a well tailored guy in the far seat in mid conversation on a car phone. From her notes, she knew that he was not the mark.

"Yes Tony, I have her now," he looked Sarang up and down. "yea, she look better than good, Boss, you're gonna have a real time." He said. After a few more moments of conversation he ended the call.

Sarang sat back and relaxed. In the backseat only sat her and the guy that was on the phone. The big Italian security was seated in the front seat with the driver. Salvatore, was the man that shared the same space with Sarang. He was Tony's under Boss and second in command. The thirst in his eye was evident as Sarang noticed him moving closer toward her.

In her mind Sarang knew if Salvatore tried anything she would have to comply or possibly blow her cover. It came with the profession.

Salvatore wanted badly to penetrate her but decided against it. He didn't want Tony to know she was tampered with before he had his way with her. He'd paid a lot of money on his sexual escapades, knowing this, Salvatore decided to take a different route.

The stocky Italian in front noticed Salvatore inch closer and tried to watch but the window divider raised, terminating all visual.

"So, how you doing, Sweetheart?" Salvatore spoke in a heavy Italian accent.

Sarang smiled, continuing to act oblivious to the language. Salvatore decided to cut the small talk, he knew a conversation would get him nowhere. Getting straight to it, he pulled his limp manhood out, laying it on his upper thigh.

Sarang tried to ignore the gesture by placing her attention to the window, watching the world go by. Salvatore wasn't having that, he grabbed her arm to get her attention as he slowly stroked himself, then told her to suck it, with verbal and hand motions.

She took a big breath, swallowed her pride placing her head in between his lap. Wrapping her lips around his small tool, it grew slightly as the blood rushed through it. She put on a show as she pulled it out her mouth, kissing it then relaxed her throat muscles in preparation to deep throat the Underboss.

She devoured it all.

His member didn't even make it far enough for her gag. Sarang sucked up and down, touching the base each time. Salvatore grabbed her head and pumped her face vigorously as if he was sexing her face. After he came in her mouth without warning, he tossed her five hundred dollars and casually got on his cellular.

Sarang wiped her mouth and spoke softly in her native tongue. "You dead, coming soon. " Then smiled at him.

CHAPTER 15

BOWIE, MARYLAND

"Here we are, Your Majesty." Solo smirked looking toward the back seat. As the window divider slid down in the expensive Bentley, his smile began to evaporate. In front of him was a silver platter that held a Smith & Wesson .45 caliber revolver, a hand cannon.

Yuki extended her and. "Maxell Strickland, kill him, quietly of course...I don't have all day."

With bugged like eyes , he replied. "Quietly?! With that?'

He nodded to the weapon in front of him.

Solo looked around for the first time actually noticing the area he was in. the neighborhood was not where he expected to be doing Fate's obligations. Many thoughts consumed his mind. He wasn't an assassin, wasn't even a killer. He grew up in the ghetto, been through a few shoot outs but never straight up murder. He was now regretting his previous choices.

Yuki became impatient. "You hear me! Be quick and leave NO witnesses, fate has spoken." Yuki narrowed her eyes.

Solo took a deep breath, grabbed the gun, tucked it in his slacks then exited the car. As soon as the door was closed, a bald eagle landed on the hood of the car instinctively making solo jump.

"Oh snap!," He tried to shoo the big bird away but it didn't even take a step back. "Yea okay, be here when I get back." Solo bucked, taunting the eagle.

Unbeknownst to Solo, as soon as he turned toward the house, the eagle transformed into a cat jumping through the sun roof landing on Yuki's lap. Solo was nervous during his approach toward the town home. It was quiet. There he was in a suburban neighborhood where the grass was green in every yard. The lawn had the same patterns as if the same guy maintained each residents yard. He didn't know if this was a test, his mind was made up, failure was not an option.

In the back of his head Solo always wondered what the gun range training was for, now he knew. 'FATE SEEKER HUH, I GUESS MR. MAXWELL'S TIME IS UP, OR FATE SAID SO' Solo thought, creeping around the back of the house. He decided since the area was so open, he would just walk like he belonged.

The guy had a deck.

'SWEET!'

Solo climbed the steps and was in front of a glass door. He looked through and didn't see anybody. He pulled his gun out, turning it around holding it like a hammer, then was about to smash the glass until an eagle landed on the deck rail and made a screeching sound forcing Solo to turn around and lower his gun.

"Yo, what's up with you, Bird?" Solo said to the eagle as it looked at him then turned its head sideways. "Whatever."

He turned his attention back to the door and decided to see if it was open.

It slid right open.

"Hmmm, whatda y'kno, this dude cant be Black up in this piece unless he, um, too comfortable."

Inside the house, he walked checking every room on the ground floor. It was empty. He opened the basement door with his sleeves and crept down stairs. The house looked brand new but with each step there was a creaking sound.

Searching the basement he came up short. "NOT A SOUL DOWN THERE EITHER?!' Headed back upstairs Solo stood at a flight of stairs that led to the second floor. From the top of the stairwell Solo herd a continuous noise.

"Max wait, ummm, w-wait a minute," A sweet voice moaned. Solo crept step by step.

"Shut up whore! take Daddy dick!!"

The sounds of lovemaking increased.

"Oh my God! I'm cu-cu-cumming!!!" The feminine voice panted.

Solo now stood at the bedroom door that the sounds of sex were coming through. He pulled his gun out holding it to his chest and took a deep breath.

"You still talking shit!" Max pumped harder.

"St-stop baby, I wanna taste you, let me taste all of you!" She begged.

Solo opened the door slowly. Max didn't even notice the gun pointed behind his head.

The girl did,

"Oh my God!" She screamed as she crab walked quickly to the back of the bed placing her back against the headboard. Maxwell was stunned to silence as he turned around putting his hands to the sky.

"Quiet now, huh?"Solo aimed his gun. "you didn't even get to finish did you?"

"Wha- what do you want?"

'Go ahead and finish," Solo waved the gun pointing to the girl," cause this is gonna be your last piece of ass you get in this lifetime."

"No wait! I g-got money!" He pleaded. "I will g-"
BOOM BOOM!!

"Ahhhhhh!" The woman screamed as brain fragments splashed on her face and chest as the barrel smoked.

"Guess you didn't want to get that last one off," Solo said to the corpse. The woman continued to scream, "Shut da' fuck up!"

"Please don't kill me! I don't even know him," She cried hysterically. "He paid me."

"Sorry, Cutie, guilty by association, no loose ends."

BOOM BOOM!

On the way to the door, Solo looked to see he only had two rounds left. He dumped the last rounds in Max for good measure.

It's never personal, it's Fate."

CHAPTER 16

NEW YORK CITY

Pulling up to Tony's house, which was located up-town in Harlem, Sarang was escorted by Salvatore through the front doors.

'TWO AT THE ENTRANCE' Sarang noted.

The house was massive. It could be considered a mansion in the state of new York. Coming through the door it seemed as the home expanded. The stairs were on both sides forming a U shape leading to the next floor. The house was laid out for a man with money. It had floor to ceiling windows on the ground level, from what Sarang could make out.

Headed up the stairs, she didn't get a chance to view the rest of what the first floor had to offer. She was uncertain of how many men actually were down there. Making it to the top, she was escorted down a hallway passing four rooms in total to her left and right.

The master bedroom was directly in front of her. Two more men stood in front of the door with automatic suppressed assault rifles. Sarang eyed the weapons, plotting her escape. The double doors opened simultaneously and there he stood.

Tony Ramos. Her target.

With a big smile, a silk robe and some tight leopard print Speedos, he welcomed Sarang with opened arms. Sarang gave Tony a bow with a smile. he enjoyed the gesture as he did the same with a knowing smile as to what was about to go down. Walking toward Tony her heels 'click-clacked' with each step against the marble floors.

The doors were closed by the security team and locked as she kept walking which put a smile on her face. At first she was just going to kill him and hit a window for her great escape, but to her discomfort the room was windowless. Sarang blew a sigh knowing she had to perform the act of sex until a exit route formed in her head.

Tony stared with lust in his eyes. Sarang's legs seemed long and glistened as he watched her skirt rise and fall with each step. Making it close enough to be grabbed, Tony, without invitation, placed his lips against hers greedily as he forced his tongue down her throat. His hands moved up her skirt grabbing a nice size plump petite round buttock cheek in thongs.

Sarang smelled great in his embrace. He cupped her B-cup breast and aggressively squeezed. Tony then pulled her tight tee over her head exposing her perky breasts. With no bra, her breasts high on her chest, no sag, with gum drop nipples. Tony moved her slowly toward the bed positioning her doggy style, but made her keep the skirt and heels on.

Tony was in heaven. Sarang's love tunnel was tight, phat and wet. It had been a long time since she was actually penetrated so she decided to make the best out of the encounter. He neared his manhood toward her canal and entered.

"Ummmm" Sarang moaned. She heard of sex but never actually felt the real thing. apart of her training was to get penetrated for reasons like this, the job.

The thickness of Tony had her surprisingly moaning loud as she bit her bottom lip to contain the guilty pleasure, "aaaa-aaahhh!!!" She panted as Tony thrust into her feeling her body with every inch he had to offer.

He kept his pace, in and out, in and out with her moistness dripping off him as he pulled out flipping her around tossing her on her back. Sarang was leaned against a bundle of pillows with her knees in her chest with a leaking love button.

"Tst, Ima show you why I'm the Boss!" Tony taunted with a thick accent as he positioned himself between her thighs.

Thrust continued in the missionary position. He wasn't making love, he was trying to put it on her. Tony was going crazy as Sarang matched his stroke with her own agenda in mind. "This bitch a freak!" He said to himself but loud enough to be heard as he slipped two fingers in her rectum.

They sweated and body rocked for the better of a hour, switching angles and positions until Tony exploded. After his eruption they laid on the bed while he smoked a cigar, satisfied that his money was well spent.

Sarang was exhausted as well, but quickly regained her composure as the mission at hand came to mind. Getting up, Tony smacked her butt.

"Let me ah, use the bathroom, then ah, it's on for dee' next round." He said, walking to the bathroom.

As the door closed, Sarang jumped off the bed looking for a weapon. Then she realized her custom chopsticks were criss-crossed in the back of her bun. Noticing her hair was already down, she jumped back on the bed frantically searching for them but couldn't find them.

Looking under the bed with her feet to the sky she located them both. Wrapping her hair she placed one of them in her hair and kept one in her hand as she put her shirt over her head.

Creeping to the bathroom door, she leaned against it and listened. Tony was singing, a flush of the toilet then water running behind it let her know he was about done. The door swung open and Tony was singing, not even noticing her behind the door. He stopped in his tracks in confusion when he noticed she wasn't there.

Not wanting to underestimate Tony as she did Choppa last time, she brandished both daggers as she crept behind Tony. He thought it was a game of hide and seek as he began to tip-toe. "Sexy laaaady... you hiding from me?" he said in a playful tone looking around. He turned around to his last expression of fear as it etched his face.

With a precision move the dagger slit his throat muting any sound from leaving his mouth as the other dagger was jammed into Tony's forehead through is skull and out the back. Falling to his knees, Sarang stood in front of him.

"You were great, what a waste." She kicked him flat to the ground as she retrieved her chopsticks out his head wiping the blood off in his chest then expertly wrapped her hair back into a bun with her chopsticks.

Sarang didn't know how much time she had before his goons would come back to check on him. She picked him up, carrying him to the bathroom and threw him in the spacious Jacuzzi turning it on high, letting it fill up and flood as it washed her juices off him.

Closing the bathroom door, Sarang walked to the bedroom door and opened it. Both goons looked her up and down but only one spoke, "Where's Tony?"

"He say alcohol, give me." Sarang said in broken English and pointed to the bathroom.

One goon walked pass and headed to the bathroom. After he turned the corner, which was a few steps from the door, Sarang turned her attention to the other good and smiled.

In the same second she punched him in his throat with a right hand as she grabbed his gun off his shoulder. the force from the punch sent him flying into the hallway. Chambering a bullet, she squeezed a round that caught up to the goon before he landed and pierced his skull with a smoking hole in the center of it. Peeking around the corner, Sarang saw the goon about to grab the door handle of the bathroom. As he grabbed it, a bullet came through the back of his head forcing his body to slide down the door.

Sarang headed to the bedroom entrance where she noticed three more goons running up the stairs. She looked down the hall.

'BRRRRAT! BRRRATTT!!!

SHOTS!

It chipped away at the door as she pulled her head back for cover. Leaning back to avoid the gunfire, she took a deep breath and did a quick analyze of the situation.

'BRRRAT! BRAAATT!!

Automatic gunfire took attempts at her flesh. Different voices could be heard , but one stuck out to her. "You have nowhere to go, Bitch! Show me your hands now!" Salvatore screamed in a heavy accent.

Sarang smiled.

That's all she needed to motivate her.

His voice.

A source to concentrate on. His disrespect fueled her senses as his voice became her new target.

Sarang walked back further into the room, backpedalling to retrieve the other gun the goon had. Now she was locked and loaded with two sub machine rifles looking like Lara Croft. She came back to the door, wielding both rifles from the hip in semi-automatic spurts.

Precision.

Head and body shots hit each goon. She watched each one fall, dead instantly upon contact before their bodies hit the ground.

More goons came!

Her speed and agility was amazing as she ran on the sides of the wall shooting and plucking them off one by one. Salvatore paused in his tracks.

"What the fuck!?" He began shooting at her as he he ran in the opposite direction, "Somebody kill her!!" He screamed as a few more goons came from different areas of the ground floor. Salvatore continued to shoot upward as he made it to the lower level.

Dropping the two empty weapons and picking up two more from fallen goons in her path, she jumped over the rail shooting at the goons as they climbed the horseshoe staircase. By the time she landed, both barrels were smoking and both of Salvatore's legs had holes in them forcing him to the ground.

Most goons were dead. The others took flight after realizing she wasn't just no foreign escort, but a trained killer. Sarang walked slowly toward Salvatore as her heels made the only noise in the house.

"Hello, Salvatore," She spoke perfect English with a devilish grin. "You thought you wasn't going to pay?"

"Fuck you, Slut! How did my kids taste, Bitch!"

Sarang chuckled. "Not as good as this gonna feel." She leaned over and pulled Salvatore's pants off exposing his genitals. She reached to grab it and began to stroke him seductively and asked, "Can I taste your kids, again?"

He spit on her. "you're gonna pay for this. Do you know who we are!" He threatened.

With his manhood in her hand, she gripped it. "So is that a yes or a no?" She leaned in closer to get eye to "eye" with it as her tongue turned into a snakes tongue with the slits and hissed. Discreetly she reached for her hair with the other hand.

"Fuck you!" He yelled

" No Thank you but you'll take some head!" She said slicing his penis completely off in a quick cut across the base.

Salvatore's screamed was piercing!

"Shut up and open your mouth. Say ahhh! " She said forcing his mouth open.

He passed out.

'SMACK!'

Sarang brought him back to his senses as he blinked a few times gagging. His hands tightly confined with his own neck tie, his manhood in his own mouth with Sarang hand covering his mouth.

"Shut up! Don't talk. I thought you Italians had manners, don't talk when there's food in your mouth." Sarang said as she stabbed him repeatedly in his heart. As his life left his body, she stood. "Think it was time for you to close that window outside your eyes."

CHAPTER 17

MONTHS LATER

Onyx and Teddy were enjoying the day. It was hot and the humidity was at its worse. Summertime in the 'hood had its advantages, but only when it came to the females in the males opinions. they wore basically nothing and left little to the imagination.

There was a neighborhood pool; it was ghetto. It barely kept a lifeguard on duty. If you couldn't swim, you better not get in the water. Both of them laid on chairs as kids ran past ignoring the don't run signs. It was a sight to see as they watched different woman get out of the water and pull wedges out their behinds.

The projects they lived in were heavily patrolled. Law enforcement was everywhere making their presence known just because they could. Most had the assumption that if you lived here, you were up to no good.

To stay out of the officers way, the pool was the location and perfect getaway for the time being. It was out of the center of the hood but still in the hood. The pool was gated which made it visible to your surroundings.

"Aye, Fat Boy, you heard from Solo today?" Teddy asked.

"Nope, not sure since yesterday, he probably at work." Onyx said. "I went by his crib this morning, Mom dukes said he didn't even come in last night."

"Is that right? He might got caught up in some girl last night."

Onyx shook his head and shot down the comment. " Nah' his girl gone back to school, remember."

"Fool I aint say his girl, I said some girl, y'kno, like a random. I swear that dude need to get a phone," Teddy stood up, "You ready to roll out? Them peoples should be gone for a few." He said referring to the police.

" Hell yeah, I'm ready. Cant get no money watching these broads walk around. They aint even swimming." Onyx got up as well.

Walking down the path of the pool, Onyx saw this girl that always tried to play thing with him, not giving him the time of day. He had an idea, "The swimming pool for swimmers!" he shouted as he pushed the girl into the water. Teddy saw the move and pushed her friend in the water as well. "Get you some!"

They jogged off as the girls swam to the rail cursing them out. Making it outside of the pool area the next destination was undecided. Coming through a cut, they noticed Solo's motorcycle in the parking lot. From what his mom told Onyx Solo didn't come home last night and the bike was parked there all night.

They chilled in the parking lot, Teddy leaned on a parked car to roll a blunt. Onyx was on the look out for a sale. After a few transactions and all the marijuana was gone, they were on cloud nine in their own worlds. The moment was short lived when an all black McLaren pulled into the lot, breaking their thoughts.

"Ooooo weee!" Teddy eyed the car with squinted eyes as it came to a slow creep pulling along side Solo's bike.

"That's a sexy ass car right there." Onyx tried to look through the five percent tints,

They stood tall from the leaning position and began to walk toward the car that sat idle for a little over two minutes. The awe of the vehicle soon turned into suspicion as Teddy began to reach for his pistol.

The eagle flew low almost hitting Teddy as the driver's door opened. "Chill, Big Boy!" Solo said, not even noticing the giant bird fly past. Usually Solo tried to avoid letting his friends see him in his work attire but time was not on Yuki's side today so he didn't have a choice.

He looked real suave. His suit was tailored from a Tom Ford collection and some Cartier frames complimented his face. With a Kodak smile, Solo looked at Teddy. "Stand down it's only me."

Teddy gave a knowing smile. "Bruh, I don't know what kind of secret job you got James Band, but I know it aint just driving, pulling up in shit like this. These last couple months you been winning and I want in."

"No bullshit, Bro! Put your dudes on." Onyx countered.

Solo began to dap his friends up as the back door slowly opened. They all looked back to notice some long sexy legs in a pair of red bottom heels extend out the car and land firmly on the concrete.

Yuki stood.

With wide frame glasses she lowered them to look at Solo's friends. "Sorry boys, I'm not hiring at the time, but Ill keep the both of you in Fates eyes," Solo blew a sigh as she continued. "But Mr. Solo, Ill call you in the morning, don't be late," She said raising her glasses walking to the driver's seat and getting behind the wheel. "Bye Boys."

Teddy and onyx looked on, staring with their mouths open in awe of her beauty. Yuki pulled off headed down the parking lot as both of them went to the middle of the lot waving wildly.

"Damn, Bro, She sexy as hell," Teddy said. "That's your Boss, Cuz?"

"Yea Brody, and she don't play no games."

Onyx walked to Solo, placing his arm around his shoulder. " I see she got you looking the part."

"Lookin' sweet, huh?" He smiled, "lookin' how I'm lookin'." His arms were extended, presenting himself like a present.

"Yea Bro, you did dat." Onyx confirmed.

"Preciate that, Playa, but now it's time to get up outta this shit." Solo said walking toward his house.

They both followed behind him. Nearly everyone in the neighborhood did a double look after noticing Solo's appearance. A few neighbors gave him praises, complimenting him on his sharp attire. He enjoyed each one of them, it was something different.

As their walk continued, the conversation flowed about nothing in particular as they made it to his front door. Solo opened the door and walked in with his friends right on his heels.

The first person he saw was his little brother. they rivaled each other back and forth pranking each other when possible. Riley was watching cartoons on TV, he was really tuned in that he didn't even look back as Teddy and Onyx sat on the couch behind him.

Solo motioned Teddy to give him the pillow that rested behind him. After catching it he threw it at Riley's head with great force. Not thinking of his gifts, the power behind the throw was strong. As it hit him, the force after it connected made Riley do a couple front summersaults until the entertainment system stopped him, leaving his feet in the air facing the ceiling.

"Owww!," Riley moaned as he rolled over holding his head, "I hate you!"

"Damn!" Teddy said covering his mouth slightly. "Why you hit that boy like dat'!"

"He know why." Solo said walking to the kitchen as Valerie came around the corner hearing the ruckus.

"Solo! You better leave my baby alone before--" Valerie started to scold him until she was in the presence of her eldest son. "Oh my goodness. Look at you. You look so handsome in your suit, "She complimented, "That new job must be treating you well, Son," She hugged him then let him go, "Don't you go messing it up!" her finger poked his forehead.

"Thanks, Ma. Ill be back, 'bouta go change up outta these work clothes."

Climbing the stairs, Solo entered his room. He looked in the mirror admiring his looks. Emptying his pockets he tossed it's contents onto the dresser. taking off his shirt, he thought he was seeing things. In the mirror he could have sworn he'd just seen Sarang sitting on his bed. He turned around to confirm his suspicions.

WHOP!

Sarang was in his face, connecting a jab to his chest. He and Sarang had a love/hate relationship. He actually wouldn't mind making her his, but she was crazy to say the least, his opinion. That attribute attracted him and scared him away at the same time.

Holding his chest, leaning on the dresser, he caught his breath, "What the hell you doing here, Woman?" he stood up tall. "I told you to stop putting yo' hands on me or Ima forget you a girl."

Sarang laughed. "Yea, okay."

"Y'know, if you wanted to see me, i could have been laying here waiting on you dipped in butter, feel me?" Solo smiled as Sarang rolled her eyes.

From downstairs Solo heard his mother yell, "Don't be stomping in my house, up there making all that noise."

Solo put a finger on Sarang's's lips, shushing her, before he responded to his mother, "My bad, Ma!"

Sarang smacked his hand down, then kicked him making him fly into the head board, landing on his bed.

Sarang walked over to his bed and sat at the foot. he rolled over to face her. "Okay, keep thinking I'm playing with you. I'm tryna be your friend but you making it hard."

Staring into his eyes Sarang spoke. "You want a friend, get a dog. Tonight you have a job. I would do it myself but I feel it's more in your comfort zone."

"Why is that?" Solo asked snatching the itinerary.

"You people like clubs, party scene not me, easy job for you."

"You people?" Solo acted offended, turning his neck to the side awaiting a response.

Sarang didn't understand his body language, so she continued to explain the details of the mission as she stood and began pacing. Solo was a little irritated. It seemed as if he was never off; never had a chance to get a break.

His body count was high, he was numb to the job and it came easy. When Sarang suggested he bring his friends to the club to make it neutral, he agreed to the favor.

She presented it as if he had a choice when in all actually he didn't in Sarang's eyes. Yuki gave him permission to go get fresh and use any car he wanted for the night.

A win, win.

Sarang saw his mind drift and brought him back. "Under no circumstance should your friends know what's going on or as you know, they will be taken care of. Remember, when you come to the mansion, make sure you're alone, Warkarmashta?" She asked if he understood.

"I got you Boo," He turned his back to her looking in the closet, "but why Yuki didn't tell-" He turned back around with a shirt in his hand to find Sarang gone. He blew a sigh. "There she go wit' dat' Batman shit."

CHAPTER 18

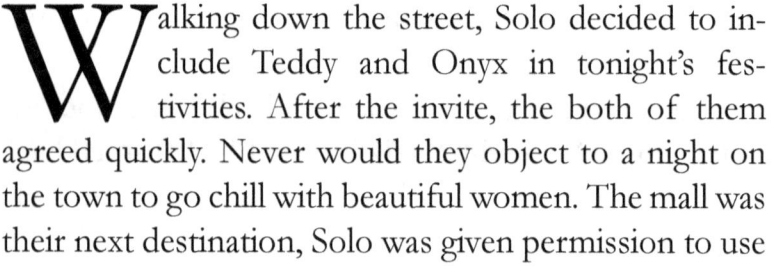

Walking down the street, Solo decided to include Teddy and Onyx in tonight's festivities. After the invite, the both of them agreed quickly. Never would they object to a night on the town to go chill with beautiful women. The mall was their next destination, Solo was given permission to use his platinum card to foot the bill and make the night as easy as possible.

"Oh yeah, you ballin' like that," Teddy said slapping high fives's with Onyx. " We 'bout to put a dent in that card."

"Not ballin', Homes, just got a nice bonus in my check so I decided to share it with my team," Solo tried to downplay the situation. Really without the card his account from the new job had him comfortably sitting on a few hundred thousand dollars.

"Shit, I don't care where it came from. You aint gotta convince me to spend your money. Let's hurry up and get on this train before you have a change of heart." Onyx said wrapping his arm around Solo's shoulder.

Making their way toward the train station, Solo felt his body tense up and his senses heighten. pausing for a second he looked to a sound in the sky. Something wasn't right. Solo had been working so hard that he was out of the loop of his neighborhoods latest beef. Teddy and Onyx had a feud with a few guys a couple weeks ago and placed a couple of them in the hospital.

Quickly Solo's attention was diverted from the sky to the corner as a car turned unto their street. It was a crown Victoria on a slow creep. It was a little past a half block and coming.

Solo zoomed in.

His sight evolved, he could now see through solid objects. Looking through the car he noticed there was four occupants in the vehicle strapped with three handguns and a pump action rifle.

Weighing his options, he didn't want to blow his cover doing something that obviously wasn't ordinary. Quickly a plan came to play. Knowing Teddy carried a pistol on him, Solo scanned his body discreetly and found its resting place on Teddy's hip.

The car neared. Teddy and Onyx were in conversation not even paying any attention. Solo pushed Teddy to the ground with one hand and lifted his shirt with the other, snatching the pistol out. It was a nine millimeter that held seventeen shots.

Onyx looked at Solo confused as he held the gun. Solo screamed. "Get down, Big Boy!" he jumped on top of the parked car in front of him.

BOC! BOC!

Solo shot at the windshield of the approaching car. The shots cracked and shattered the window but didn't break it. Running from car roof to car roof of the parked cars, he continued to fire. He shot with rapid fire first hitting the driver. The car swerved and crashed.

The passenger and one of the backseat passengers returned fire as Solo jumped off the car landing on the sidewalk. With his back pressed against a car, he looked down the street to see Teddy and Onyx kneeling a few lengths back.

SHOTS!

MORE SHOTS!

Bullets pierced the car Solo hid behind. Thinking of his next move, he grabbed a mirror off the car. An idea came to mind. Solo tossed the mirror high in the sky. With his unique vision he looked at the images of the shooters as the mirror rotated, pinpointing their exact location.

Rising from his crouched position, Solo fired his weapon with precision. Two shots to the head dropped the shooters where they stood. Solo looked around the car to locate the final shooter and spotted him running in the opposite direction down the street about to turn the corner.

Solo took aim.

He blew a sigh lowering his gun. He decided to let him go. "Next time, Guy." He thought as Onyx and Teddy ran up behind him.

"Damn, Cuz, you like that!," Teddy massaged Solo's shoulders excited. "That was like some John Wick shit!"

Solo inhaled then exhaled a few breaths then relaxed his shoulders as his heart rate started to minimize its rapid beat. He looked at Onyx with narrowed eyes. "Yo, who the fuck was them dudes?" Solo knew it had something to do with Onyx. He's the hot-headed one. When Teddy has a problem, he excitedly tells the team what's going on, whereas Onyx thinks he could handle any and all problems himself.

Onyx waved him off. "Fuck that shit, Homie. They aint here no more, it's the life." He replied, shrugging his shoulders.

Teddy shook his head. "The life? What life? Life as them bodies that don't have any left," he pointed to the dudes laid out on the street. "Or life as in a beautiful future."

He said looking to the sky.

"Hmph, both I guess. Just depends what end of the stick you get, y'digg."

Solo began to walk. It always irritated him when Onyx downplay's real life situations and experiences. He had a nonchalant attitude about everything, good or bad.

Ditching the train idea, they headed back to their neighborhood. Solo slid through his phone looking for contacts but came up empty. Sirens could be heard in the distant but close vicinity. Wouldn't anybody with a car answer his phone call. He contemplated on taking Yuki up on her offer for a while about the vehicles right now instead of later, but he would have to ditch his friends to go to the estate, so settled for an U.ber.

CHAPTER 19

THE FATELANDS

S arang walked through the hallways of the estate getting herself ready to shadow Solo on his newly adopted Calling. Covered in a towel, a whirlwind of air by-passed her as she turned the corner to notice Yuki enter the only black door in the dwelling.

Yuki sat in her fortress of solitude. It was a restricted area for the other seekers. The Death room. A name the seekers called it amongst themselves. Yuki was the only person allowed entry in this section of the domain besides one other seeker.

Inside this room, behind the black door, was a mystical pond that stretched the length of the room. At the foot of the pong was an inch of water. The further you walked the more the pond defied the laws of physics as it quickly deepened. Yuki stood looking over the pond, she let her robe fall. The chill from the room stiffened her nipples.

Her body was flawless. Her skin had a natural shine as if she were covered in moisturizing oils. Her breasts sat high, not too big or small. A nice set of C- cups graced her chest. Yuki, being of Japanese appearance, didn't have a big rear end, but nice tear drop cheeks that fit perfectly in her size two jeans.

Letting her hair fall down her back, in front of the pond she stood eyes closed inhaling a fresh breath of air that came off the water. This was routine before she entered to retrieve Fate's Callings.

Besides Yuki, Sarang was the only other seeker that has access to this fortress. If Yuki was to be unable or dead was she only allowed to use it. Sarang was next in line to continue Fate's work.

Outlining the pond were black hairless cats that let off a pheromone that rejuvenated all senses to the max. The energy boost was needed. When traveling to the 7th dimension, everything exists. It's a world outside of all the worlds that monitors and dictates everything doing on in the galaxy.

Naked, Yuki jumped and dived into the pond. As she entered the water, it began to swirl like a tornado swallowing her body as it crystalized quickly taking her to

"The fatelands", a section of the 7th dimension were Fate's are called upon.

Everything went dark momentarily. Lights, they appeared in an instant, temporarily blinding, Yuki. She was prepared and knew the entry cycle well but it still was a surprise experience, every time.

Flashing lights.

They flickered as her vision began to stabilize and become focused on her surroundings. The Fatelands was in clear view. The ground was mushy. Yuki's toes sunk into the mud-like substance up to her ankles. The skies were the color of ash with a low red sun. The tree's, tall and wide, but the branches were naked of leaves as slight breezes of humidity swam ripples in the dry air.

It was hot.

Sweat beads dripped off Yuki's forehead as she reached for one of the torches that burned bright, letting off cool smoke, flawless skin was now rough with ridges of a serpent. Her eyes were the color of the Fatelands sun with no iris no pupil, but vision was usual, above normal in the extreme environment, but her trans formation to her natural state helped tremendously.

Yuki followed the path as random eyes appeared then quickly disappeared in different areas both high and low. A massive wolf-like beast with a human-like frame appeared standing two paws tall with a shadow that darkened all the lights.

All that was seen as it spoke in a raspy voice was it's six inch teeth. "Why are you here, Slave?"

Deathtidus stood in front of the flaming gates that just ignited as he spoke, stopping Yuki from entering. He was the gatekeeper to the only entrance and exit. No other option was available but through him.

Yuki held her stance. "I'm here from the third dimension's moos called Tierra and I need to speak to, Replica. I have concerns."

Replica was the leader of this section of the Otherworld. Usually the flaming gates would be opened, but this visit from Yuki was unannounced so Deathtidus was on on guard, unaware of her arrival.

After extensive questioning, Yuki gained entry and continued to walk the path. The mushy mud-like substance slowly turned into golden sand the closer she walked toward Replica's chambers. The torches that lined the path lost their glow and were now dim with blue lights.

"Replica, its me, Yuki," She said coming up to the empty throne. Mystical dust was surrounding the throne. It was black and started to rise forming a body as it spoke.

"Yes, my child." It took the form of Yuki in her Earthly state. Replica could take the appearance of any organism, usually It takes the form of whoever it speaks to, keeping its natural embodiment a mystery.

"Solo is learning fast, I fear a uh-"

"Resistance." Replica finished the sentence.

"Yes, I feel like the stronger he gets, the harder it will be to control him."

Replica was growing impatient. He didn't really understand the reason for Yuki's rambling. His position was to rule over the Fatelands and send out Fates callings through out the Galaxy.

Yuki grew nervous of the completion rate at which Solo was working. He became very defiant and quick. Every time they were in each others presence, Yuki could feel the energy coming off him. He was becoming powerful. Too powerful.

Replica grinned at her rants. Is she was this worried now, he definitely was going to be a problem after his first visit to the 7th dimension to level up his gifts. Replica had no worries. This information actually made its grin turn into a rare smile.

If this human had his top seeker on edge, then the idea of the recruitment program was a good idea.

"Bring him to me!" Replica demanded.

Yuki lowered her head. "Yes, Master."

Before she could even raise her head back up, the form of Yuki that Replica took turned back into a pile of black dust before her feet. A wind blew making the dust disappear leaving behind an empty throne.

Deathtidus appeared behind Yuki as she stood staring at the empty chair. "Its time." It said.

Yuki turned around and sighed. "Yea, yea, yea." Then began to walk pass the gatekeeper back down the path she just came as he disappeared before her eyes.

Sarang was in the estate. After getting her clothes on she walked down the hallway. Passing the Black door she paused and was about to open it. She knew Yuki was still in there because a bright light was shining from underneath the door. She was tempted as she reached.

Sarang was no stranger to the Otherworld. She wasn't restricted to enter, only restricted from going to the Fatelands. As her hand was about to grab the knob, it turned from the opposite end and opened.

"Yes?" Yuki stood in front of the door, closing it as she made her exit. She stood face to face with Sarang.

"Uh, nothing. Just thought you called me. I don't want anything." Sarang tried to turn on her heels headed the other way. She took two steps forward, in a flash Yuki appeared in front of her.

"Lies. You know I didn't call you from behind "that" door," She pointed to the Black one. "so what did you want?" Yuki asked with a knowing look and arms folded.

Sarang was actually human. She was unaware of this revelation. As an orphaned child, she was taken by Yuki at the tender age of two. She was taken to the 7th dimension and was raised in The Otherworld. There she grew up believing Yuki was her mother. The older she became, the stronger she got. The energy that surrounded her most of her life gave the illusion that The Otherworld was home.

This was one of the reasons Sarang thought so highly of Yuki and held her on a pedestal. In her eyes, Yuki was her mother, and like any child, she wanted to make her proud. Yuki took advantage of her oblivious mind and it worked out for the better as far as Sarang's skill set.

"I-I just saw the light and got curious."

Sarang confessed with her head down.

Even at the age of twenty-two, Yuki could still make her feel like a toddler in trouble. In the the eyes of any perpetrator, she was a fearless killer, let alone beautiful, but in the presence of Yuki, Sarang was nothing but a Fate seeker.

"Curious? You know what's behind that door. Don't start acting silly. Now go do what I told you. The guy should be at the establishment tonight and Fate needs him gone."

Originally Yuki gave the calling to Sarang, but she told Solo it was his deed to complete. She was going to shadow Solo when in all actuality it was her mission to complete. Sarang decided to keep this action away from the both of them. As long as the calling gets completed, Fate is on top and that is all that mattered.

"Ok, I'm headed out now. I need to go make some preparations as everything goes hassle free." She headed down the hall.

"Sarang!" Yuki called to her back stopped her in mid stride not looking back. "When you see Solo, tell him I need to see him."

Sarang nodded her understanding and continued to walk. She didn't have anywhere she needed to be right now, it was still early in the afternoon. The mall sounded like a good idea and the thought was dancing in her head. Standing outside the estate, Sarang inhaled a breath of air. Today was a decent day. The sun was shining with not a cloud in sight. Blue skies could be seen for miles with slight breeze that barely made the leaves shake.

Looking down the stairs that led to the driveway, a car set with the door wide open. A maid stood beside it with the keys in hand and a gold platter with a chrome compact .40 caliber Glock. Sarang smiled at the sight of the sun glistening off the pistol as she went down the steps and retrieved the contents off the platter.

Sitting in the car, she pressed the start button and the car growled to life. Yuki's Audi Sport was her choice to drive. Sarang loved the handle of the car, the interior was a plus. Pink. It was her favorite color. She was a girly girl at heart but hid it well from everyone, especially Yuki. It was a sign of weakness.

Cruising down the street, she drove with not a care in the world. In the car she had many thoughts of which mall she wanted to shop at and what to buy. Really nothing was needed. She owned everything she wanted, but when she gets bored she either goes shopping or training. Today she chose to shop.

Parking in the lot, she grabbed her pistol, placed it in her purse and began to walk the length of the parking lot.

CHAPTER 20

The U.ber driver never came. Once they realized the area, it was a declined fare. Four more drivers followed suit and didn't want to take the risk. It wasn't surprising but still unexpected. Usually cabs would be the ones to turn their nose up in the neighborhood, now apparently U.ber had its reservations.

Solo and the crew walked back to their projects. They had to find another means of transportation. Teddy had an idea. "Ima go see if I could grab Mom's car."

Solo laughed at the thought. "You know yo' momma aint 'bout to let you get that car, especially cause of what you did lat time."

"You cant live in the past, Bro."

"I'm not but she might."

A couple weeks prior, Teddy borrowed his mother's car so they could all attend a concert. Plied in the car were his friends along with three other females. The concert went off incident free. It was what happened after the concert that turned the night for the worst.

Headed to the hotel, the females were promiscuous and ready to have fun, or so Solo and them thought. Solo swiped his platinum card and purchased a joint room for the night. Intent on having a good time, he also paid for a few bottles of liquor before their arrival.

Things were going well for the first hour until there was a knock at the door. Solo didn't waste anytime, he had his female companion in the bathroom with him as he enjoyed her "company". Teddy opened the door, bottle in hand unaware of the immediate danger he was in.

The hairs on Solo's neck came alive as they stiffened. It alerted him as he pushed the girl out his way, opening the bathroom door. He peeked around the corner of the wall to see two masked assailants brandishing hand-guns demanding money and anything else of value.

They were caught slipping.

The would-be robbers didn't have the best intel on their caper. They were informed that Teddy and Onyx were the only two in the hotel. Solo scaled the wall as the robbers ransacked the room in search of Teddy and more valuables. Solo kneeled down grabbing a vase off the side table and threw it at the guy who held guard in the living area. The force behind the throw knocked the guy out instantly.

Surprisingly the vase didn't break. Whatever material it was manufactured with was very touch and durable. Teddy picked up the guy's gun and ran to the other guy to catch him by surprise.

SHOTS!

Solo and Onyx ran to the room where the piercing sound was heard to find the guy clutching his manhood. The would-be robber screamed in agony as he rolled around on the floor.

"Lets get outta here!" Solo suggested.

They all ran out the hotel room leaving the females behind. Making it to the parking lot, another guy was going through Teddy mother's car. He was ripping panels, cutting seats and everything in search of a come up as he frantically kept his pace.

Furious, Teddy started shooting recklessly alerting the guy who instantly stopped his search, ran to his own car a few spaces down and peeled off. They all ran to the car following Teddy to make their great escape. Surprisingly, Teddy decided to give the assailant some chase. He burst into traffic weaving in and out. He shot into traffic aiming at the other car until the clip was emptied. The driver of the other car was a better driver, he drove through traffic with ease.

The light was red.

They both ran the light!

Teddy didn't make it.

CRASH!!!

The car spun out of control after hitting another car leaving the bumper in the middle of the street as he gained control leaving the scene.

"Yeah you probably right but that's why I have a spare key," Teddy said dangling them with two fingers, "cant live in da' past, you rollin' or what?"

"So you just gonna steal your Moms shit?" Solo asked in disbelief.

"Of course not, I'm borrowing it." Teddy smiled as Onyx hopped in the front seat. Solo shook his head and followed suit.

The ride was smooth even with the few years of mileage. Teddy's mother owned a Buick and took very good care of it, that's until the accident, now it had a different color bumper that didn't match the rest of the exterior.

Arriving at the mall, the parking lot closet to the entrance was occupied. That only meant that the mall was crowded. The mall was their playground, most of the girls were there to shop, but a percentage of them were window shoppers and Teddy and onyx didn't mind paying to play.

They walked through the parking lot as if they owned the whole scene. Confidence and conceit was evident in their swagger. Tonight was going to be fun, a needed fellas night out.

It's been a while since they were able to enjoy each others company. With Solo working and being bust, he really didn't have personal time. Even though tonight would be no different, he had the opportunity to include his friends at work, unbeknownst to them, it was a calling.

Shopping wasn't a favorite thing to do amongst them. After visiting a few stores, they were satisfied with their selections as Solo footed the bill. Heading to the food court everyone brought their own meals from different food fronts.

Sitting off in the corner, Solo spotted Sarang eating a Caesar salad. An instant smile appeared naturally upon recognition. He stood up.

"Ill be back." Making his way toward her, before he could get close, she lifted her head and her eyes narrowed.

Teddy and Onyx looked on, "Look, Brah, Solo over there tryna spit game to the exotic beauty ova' there." Teddy pointed.

Solo's smile was big, Sarang frowned pushing the empty chair beside her under the table so he couldn't sit. "What you want?" Her face balled up.

"Other than you, just was wondering were you following me, " Sarang rolled her eyes at the statement. "Cause if you are, I don't mind." Solo licked his lips.

The chair that Sarang slid under the table was kicked by her, causing it to slide into Solo with force, knocking him back.

Onyx laughed, "Look look, Brah," He headed towards Solo, "Baby girl just kicked the shit out that chair into Solo!" He said excited, pointing now.

Solo rubbed his stomach. The chair hit him a little harder than he expected it would. "You can play hard to get all you want," Solo stated smiling, turning the chair around backwards taking a seat. "So, what's in da' bags?"

Sarang pulled her bags closer to her body. She was unclear to the feelings she felt around Solo. Never had she ever felt like this in The Otherworld. Emotion. The attraction was unexplainable. His presence seemed to brighten her day, but her exterior demeanor would never expose her. She wasn't transparent in that sense.

"None of your business!" She snapped standing up. "I know you better be ready for tonight, Ill be watching you."

That brightened up his smile. "Oh yea, you might as well come with me, y'kno, be my date. No need to spy." He tried to grab her hand.

Sarang couldn't understand her feelings as she almost accepted his embrace. Impulsively, she resorted to what she knew best and snatched her hand away spinning into a kick, landing square in the center of his chest as he flew three feet in the air landing at Teddy's and Onyx feet flat on his back.

"Dayum!!" They both sang in union as Teddy continued to sang, "Someone please call 9-11," A popular 90's song as Onyx picked Solo up and also commented. "Slim, she kicked the shit out you. She looked like she knew that Kung-Fu shit." He said taking a bite out of his steak and cheese sub.

Solo held his chest as he was helped up, "She likes me." He smiled.

Sarang didn't know why she just kick solo like that. It was more of an reaction if anything. Things were happening to her body that only seemed to happen around him. Her whole life she was sheltered. She never was around any men at anytime by herself except Sensei. This was foreign. Before Solo, there were only females in the mansion, so this constant contact weighed heavy.

Sarang sped through the hallway. the pace was quick as she made it to the parking lot, bags in tow. Her mind was everywhere, emotions on its own high. She had to get out of his presence.

She needed answers.

Sarang opened her car and headed back to the estate. Cruising the streets, her original destination as clouded, thoughts of the calling came to mind. Even though she pushed the weight of the deed unto Solo, it still was her calling to complete.

The next destination was the dojo. In her head, Sarang thought she might be able to kill two birds with one stone by talking to Sensei. He might be able to give his wisdom on the emotional roller coaster she had been dealing with and also get a little training in also.

Sarang skid to a stop at the Georgetown Dojo, not paying attention as her mind roamed, she nearly crashed. It seemed if the area was clear, atleast as far as she could see but it was an illusion.

Looking up at the engraved address above her head, she nearly tripped over what seemed like a body of some sort. The way it was placed on the ground bagged up, she was unable to see it before in the deepening blackness of the street.

A dark silhouette of multiple claws flew low in the shadows, it had been more than enough to keep her moving. Sarang thought it was one of Yuki's pets, spying, but it didn't look like anything she'd seem before.

Something told her to keep it moving. Sarang knew from experience that keeping in touch with one's animal instincts was vital in surviving. a little fear was a good thing, it kept her adrenaline flowing.

Entering the Dojo, Sarang called out, "Konichiwa." the melody of the greeting was soft and friendly as it echoed through out. She walked deeper into the dojo, her eyes roamed with each step. It was too quiet for her liking so she stopped and called out again, but with a little more authority.

After a brief pause a voice answered. "Hai?" It was Sensei. He appeared right behind Sarang as she spun around to acknowledge him.

"I hate when you do that," She said, head low shaking it. She don't like to get caught slipping. The relationship between the two is close. She had known him since she was five years old, her first training day. The Sensei chuckled as Sarang bowed showing her respect for her elder and much more knowledgeable. Quickly his smile turned into a straight face, emotionless. He was a serious and very deadly man. Sarang looked him over noticing his choice of apparel. All black. Usually he wears his combat training dojo.

"Hey!? Where you going?" She asked.

"Never mind that," He waved her off. "What are you doing here? Is everything okay?" Concern was heavy in his line of questioning.

Even though he had plans for today, very important ones at that, he didn't mind tending to whatever problems she might have had. He was an expert at reading body language and something was off with his student.

Sarang was hesitant. Slowly pronouncing each syllable as if it was one word Sensei said," Spil- lit."

She relented. She started with the changes in her mind, then body. She began explaining everything. Thoughts of Solo was a main topic and she'd been wondering why it was happening.

Sensei had the look of embarrassment and confusion as he intensively listened. The way Sarang was describing her emotional roller coaster, physically and emotionally was surprising to him.

"That's just your hormones raging, it's something "you humans" go through, y'know." As soon as the words left his mouth his eyes bubbled but he dared not make eye contact.

"You humans?" Sarang face was of bewilderment. She was lost for words.

Sansei turned around finally making eye contact, realizing what he had just revealed. Pandora's box was now open. He blew a heavy sigh, "Oh boy,"

Sarang began to get emotional. "What are you not telling me?" She pleaded for answers that landed on deaf ears.

"I-I cant my child, you need to talk to your...mother," He mustered up after a slight pause, "Come on, I was heading to the estate anyway. We go together, yes?"

Sarang shook her head. "Nah'. You go, I have other plans."

CHAPTER 21

"Come on, Homie, why we gotta wait here?" Teddy asked.

The shopping trip was over and they were in the Northwest section of the District. Washingtonians call it Uptown. It was the wealthiest parts of the city. Funds had to be impeccable to own a residence in this neighborhood, or area. Most had gated entry's and or security that walked the perimeter of the area keeping all trespassers at bay.

"No bullshit, Cuz, got us in this uppity ass neighborhood. Da' police would prolly' lock us up for being to sexy in this bland ass community, y'digg." Onyx said brushing his own shoulders.

"Shut the fuck up! Wit your retarded self. I told ya'll my Boss is very strict about her home. NOBODY is to come to her home or I'll get fired."

Solo left his friends at the subway station while he hailed a cab. Lucky for him there was a line of parked cabs waiting for this particular reason; people to exit the train in need of further transport.

He cruised the city streets in awe of the nice expensive luxurious homes that passes his eyes. Each seemed to be better than the next. The drive lasted about ten minutes, mainly because of traffic heading out the city. Most people that worked in the District didn't live there.

Pulling up to the security gate, Solo entered the digital passcode. The gate opened but the driver wouldn't proceed. "Go ahead, Sir. You could pull to the front." Solo said.

The driver looked through the rearview mirror and spoke, "No, no thank you. I've heard things about this residence, I'll pass. But your total amount is--"

The landing of the eagle on the hood of the cab cut his statements short. Solo looked around the seat. "That'll be how much you said?" He dug into his pocket awaiting the sum.

The eagle locked eyes with the driver, Solo never saw the eagle land. Its eyes turned red, staring daggers through the driver. It frightened him to say the least.

"Oh my God! What the hell is that?!" The driver asked Solo who in turn looked to notice a black cat on the hood.

"It's just a damn cat, Homes, chill dude."

"Get out! Get out now!" The driver panicked after seeing it transform before his own eyes.

As soon as Solo feet touched the pavement, the driver pulled off without even collecting the fare. Solo looked on as the cat jumped into his arms. "What you doing out here?" He tucked the cat and began his walk up the swirly path leading to the estate.

Climbing the stairs, Solo saw a home helper. As if on cue she came with the silver platter with multiple car keys on display but presenting them as if she was serving up his favorite dish. "Don't mind if I do." He smiled looking on the platter with multiple selections.

Behind the maid, the door to the estate opened. Yuki came out and looked Solo over. She still felt a little timid that Replica had requested his presence. "My maids aren't here for you, " Yuki stopped in front of the platter grabbing a key.

Solo lifted his his hands. "So you saying I cant grab a key?" He asked as she continued to walk down the stairs.

"Sure you could, but I need to talk to you later. Sarang didn't tell you to come over here."

"Nope! Her mind seemed to be all over the place. You know I have that effect of woman, I see it effecting you too." He said as he reached for a key smiling. It was a Bentley Continental. Usually Solo would stay away from such flashy vehicles but today was special, he was going to stunt for his friends.

"Well make sure you come back here after you do whatever it is you're about to do."

"Yes your highness."

"What!"

"My bad," Solo faced Yuki and bowed. "Hai, Oka-son." Meaning yes, mother, He stated sarcastically.

The cat jumped out of Solo's arm landing on Yuki's shoulder as she headed to an opening garage. Solo was on her heels headed to his ride for the night. Thoughts of tonight's obligations ran heavy in his mind. Headed back to the train station, he wondered how was he going to complete the mission when there for one one; his friends to consider, and secondly he couldn't bring a weapon inside. The club did full body checks and had a metal scanner.

This was going to have to be a physical take down. No telling how many of the marks friends would be accompanying him. That was another concern, then the element of not getting pointed out or caught. Needless to say, Sarang made it sound easy, but in reality it's never easy in this field of work.

"DAYUM!!" Onyx eyed the car as he ran his hand down the hood as it came to a stop. "I got shotgun!" He rushed to open the door.

Teddy smiled. He didn't mind riding in the back of this car, "Cool wit' me. You two can chauffeur me as I cool behind behind these curtains."

Solo remained quiet as the both of his friends ranted back and forth about nothing. His mind was still preoccupied with tonight's endeavors. The night was approaching. He decided to head back to his neighborhood. Usually Solo would have a complex about how he pulled up in a fancy car. Nowadays it didn't matter matter, he could careless about what people said or thought.

In the coming months Solo had a plan to move his family out of the area and putting this part of their life in the rearview. After the many completed callings, he had a couple hundred thousand dollars saved and it was his ticket out.

Solo tried to open his front door as he stood on the porch of his mother's home. It was locked.

"Shit!" He patted his pockets. During the shootout he must had misplaced the keys so he had to knock.

There were three audible knocks at the door. He made sure not to bang too loud for fear of a bad reaction from Valerie. There was silence.

"Knock again!" Onyx suggested.

"hell nah, you could knock, go ahead tough guy but make sure you stay in front of the door when you do." Solo challenged.

They waited.

In a child-like voice Riley answered, more like sung his response. "Whoooo issss it?"

Solo blew a sigh, "Open da' door, Punk!"

"Password, " Riley snickered behind the closed door. This made Solo irritated as he responded. "Stop playin' before I get mad, Riley!"

"I...said...password."

Teddy pulled Solo back. "Let me try, "Solo gave the door a slight fist bump then backed away. Riley was peeking through the peephole as he stood on his Tonka truck for height. "Hey Riley, It's me, Teddy. Can you let us in, Big Time." He smiled big as Riley looked on only seeing teeth in a circular form of the hole that he watched through.

"Sorry teddy. You guilty by association. Now if you don't mind, password, puhlease'."

Teddy looked at Solo and whispered. "How his bad ass learn that phrase?" Solo shrugged with no answer to give. teddy looked back at the door. After digging into his pocket, he retrieved a twenty dollar bill. "Is this the password?" He dangled it so it was clearly visible.

Riley smiled. It just might be, slide it under the door and take twenty steps back. Solo looks like his panties are in a bunch, " He giggled as Solo tried to rush the door but was held back by Onyx. "Make sure you hold onto Mr.. Magic Mike back there."

Teddy slid the money and Riley watched them back up. When Riley felt they were at a safe distance he unlocked the door, then bolted.

Solo's ears tingled as he heard the locks turn. Only he could hear it and began running back toward the door. Opening it, Solo saw Riley at the top of the stairs waving and dangling his new fortune. Solo squinted his eyes and began running toward his little brother. After a couple steps, it was like the room slowed up as his senses heightened.

First his nose flared and he frowned."What's that smell?" A thought to himself, then his eyes zoomed in. "What the hell baby oil doing out here?" Still in a slow motion sprint, he looked down.

Too late.

The room sped back up as he slid across the living room floor, finally crashing into a table in the kitchen flipping him over resulting in him landing on his back.

From the top of the stairs, Riley enjoyed an uncontrollable laughter that left him in tears of joy. Teddy and Onyx entered the house to see Solo slowly getting up. Teddy nudged Onyx, "His little brother crazy." He joked.

Valerie came around the corner. "What the hell you doing down there, Solo?" She stopped at the top of the stairs as Riley wrapped his arms around one of her thighs.

Solo looked to see his mother and was about to answer until he noticed Riley and smiled a devilish grin narrowing his eyes at his brother. The glare was so intense that the light above his mother's head blew out, scaring her as she jumped back. He knew he did it, just didn't know how. Yuki never told him about these "gifts" as she so elegantly proposed it.

His body had been progressing rapidly. This wasn't the first anomaly he experienced, but it was the first of many to come that shocked him silent. Valerie sent Riley to go get the broom. Solo looked at his men as they stared.

"What?!"

"I don't know why, but on everything I love, it looked like you did that that shit, I swear." Teddy raised his right hand to the sky.

Solo waved him off. "Come on." He told them to follow him to his room bags still in tow so they could chill for a while before they got dressed for the night.

Following him, the whole accusation was dropped. It was more of a joke if anything. Couldn't nobody explain it, so it didn't happen the way his eyes saw it. The reality of it, they just blamed it on the marijuana that was smoked earlier.

The bright sun in the sky disappeared, it was replaced wit a dim full moon. No stars in the sky could be seen. The air was dry as Solo inhaled a fresh breath of it. It was crunch time.

Onyx and Teddy were oblivious to tonight's events. All Solo could hear in his ears were their rants on how many females they were going to get as they all walked to the luxurious car that was parked on the lot.

Everyone was dressed to impress. The latest fashions graced their lean muscular frames as if the designer made it just for them. Solo spared no expense, not because he swiped was limitless and would be billed to Yuki.

Getting in the car, their own little party had already started. Styrofoam cups full of Patron' and blunts loaded with high quality Kush were in attendance. Chinky eyes and a slurred speech could be heard as Solo pulled off. Solo was good, he didn't know if his friends being inebriated was for the better or worse, only time would tell.

CHAPTER 22

The new found information didn't set too well for Sarang. Her mind was racing with unanswered questions. Instead of going with Sensei to the estate, she decided to follow. 'YA'LL THINK YA'LL COULD JUST TELL ME ANYTHING! TELL ME LIES! THEM INNOCENT LITTLE GIRL DAYS ARE LONG GONE. I NEED ANSWERS!'

Sarang gripped the steering wheel tightly. Keeping a safe distance, she stayed in a quiet pursuit. Something was going down and she knew it. All her years coming to the Dojo, never had she seen Sensei dressed in that type of attire or no students present. For a long time she thought the kids lived there.

To add to Sarang's suspicion, when she arrived at the Dojo, the area around it seemed weird. The shadow that flew over her head, the bulky bags that sat out front. It was to many "first" for one day and she was far from stupid or gullible to believe in coincidence, not to mention Sensei slip up, 'YOU HUMANS. SO ALL THIS TIME NOBODY WAS GONNA TELL ME, UGHHHH!' Sarang banged the steering wheel.

As she drove, Sarang noticed Sensei wasn't going to the estate. This new turn of events had her more interested. To find out another side of his life style could be a revelation.

The drive was becoming a lengthy one. Exhaustion started to take its effect. No longer was she in the city. Country roads and farmlands were in clear site. Neighbors a half mile from one another. The area was not familiar, but she was determined to keep up. Even as the sun descended and light turned into darkness, her motivation was high.

So little time and too many things to get done. Sensei finally stopped as Sarang continued to ride by. Noticing the layout of the property, she came to the conclusion that it was someone's residence that was well kept.

Glancing in the driveway, Sarang saw there were only two cars parked, including the one Sensei just exited. This country-side home was massive. Confusion broke all the the barriers of logic as Sarang pulled to the side of the road trying to piece together some type of summary of the sight she just saw.

"You slipping Ol' Man." Yuki hugged Sensei.

"No I'm not. I already noticed your daughter following me the whole time. I let her. She has some questions. I may have accidently informed her of her humanity."

"What!" She screamed as her natural form tried to come through the mask of her earthly features.

This was unexpected. The meeting was supposed to be about a whole different subject. That comment had Yuki slightly side tracked but quickly recovered. After a sigh and a wave of her hand, she decided to deal with Sarang whenever she decides to make her presence known. There were more threatening problems at hand that needed to be tended to.

Yuki explained to Sensei that a portal was open and a couple of the 7Th dimensions creatures escaped and needed to be apprehended before they reeked havoc on Earth.

The conversation went on for a while. Debating different solutions didn't come easy with two alpha assassins. Sarang was far off, lamped in the creases listening to every word spoken about the escapees.

'NOW IT ALL MAKE SENSE. THE CREEPY SHADOW THAT HOVERED AROUND THE

DOJO. I KNEW IT DIDNT BELONG' Sarang thought.

She wanted to interject and tell them her thoughts. But after thinking for a moment, she realized how frivolous that would be and if she did, it would be exposing herself informing them that she was spying when she wasn't even suppose to there.

'I'LL LET THEM DEAL WITH IT. I HAVE OTHER THINGS OF MORE IMPORTANCE TONIGHT.'

Sarang looked at her watch and noticed it was late. Solo had to be in the club or on his way. If this calling was not completed correctly, it would be her to deal with the consequences.

Failure was not an option.

Deciding to leave well alone, she placed her car in gear and seconds later was driving pass the house, headed to the city. Sarang had a job to ensure. Getting it don't swiftly with out incident was the goal.

"Ill see you later...mother." Sarang drove in silence.

CHAPTER 23

S olo and his crew were enjoying a good time at the function. The club was a new hot spot. It was normal for the lines to wrap around the corners well after 12:00 am. The night was still young in the minds of all the partygoers even though it was 12:45am. Solo has a plan, but was yet to spot his victim for tonight. Fate had its deadlines and it was closing in.

Tonight's performance grew a large crowd. R&B's queen B was supposed to have an appearance. Her presence alone brought out all the beautiful woman who were swaying their hips to the beat of her songs and enjoying the vibes that surrounded them.

Hip Hop, Pop, and Reggae made the floors vibrate. Conversation was nearly impossible as the bass transgresses. Lights of all colors reflected off the surrounding mirrors on the wall causing a light show illusion. Hands fist pumped and waved back and forth in the crowd. Solo looked up from his drink after it was empty.

Then he saw her...

The bar was stationed in the back of the club. Occupants on the stools has a clear view of the entire establishment. Sarang sat observing, making sure all was well from afar. Many guys tried to get her attention but it wasn't working. She ignored them and kept watch, she was an extra set of eyes, if needed. her outfit was form fitting on her lean but eye popping frame. The look made for constant contact. Her dress, red, with a long slit stopping at the entry of her fruit garden. Her legs, long sexually muscular and tone. A body of a temptress, but she didn't entertain any of the advances that were attempted.

Her eyes were glued on Solo, watching him watch everybody else. Sarang was yet to find the mark as of yet, she began to question the instructions, then the thought left. The itinerary said he would be there, so it was facts without a shadow of a doubt.

Patience, a hard pill to swallow at times. Sarang drank another shot, Patron' was her poison, she loved the sensation on her throat after a swallow from the short bottle.

The mark entered the club.

Sarang looked toward Solo who was frozen still. The look on his face was that of a ghost. Teddy noticed the change in his friends demeanor and followed his gaze.

"Shit...," Teddy said tapping Onyx. "...aint that Ebony over there?"

"Damn Bruh, sure is. We gotta go grab Solo before Ol' boy she with get his ass stomped in here."

Ebony was Solo's girlfriend from his neighborhood. It was a complicated relationship between the two. Ebony was supposed to be at school, but here she was, in the club with Solo's mark. His emotions ran high. Solo became numb. What was at first business just turned personal in that moment. Sarang jumped off the bar stool, moving swiftly toward Solo. She noticed something...

Onyx and Teddy reached Solo. "Hey, Big Guy, you good?" Onyx grabbed Solo by the shoulder.

Solo was heaving. Anger made his heartrate quicken as he responded. "No," never looking back but smacking Onyx's arm of his shoulder almost knocking him down.

Ebony was smiling hard, listening to whatever that was being whispered in her ear. She locked eyes with Solo and her smile disappeared as her pupils widened.

...Sarang's eyes widened. That was the first time she'd ever seen this happen. Looking back at Solo's hand, he had it in a fist. What surprised Sarang was the size of it. It was three times its normal size. It could be mistaken for the Incredible Hulk's, except his was brown not green.

Sarang yelled, "Solo, noooo!"

CHAPTER 24

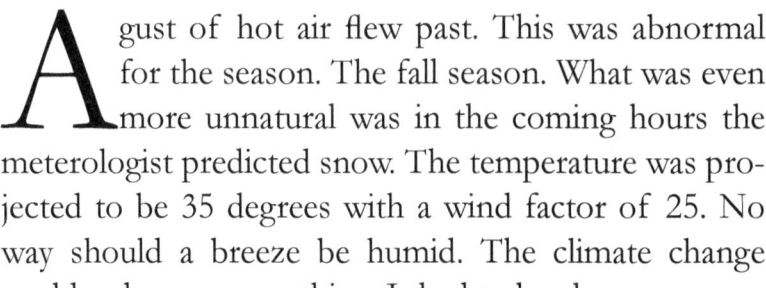

A gust of hot air flew past. This was abnormal for the season. The fall season. What was even more unnatural was in the coming hours the meterologist predicted snow. The temperature was projected to be 35 degrees with a wind factor of 25. No way should a breeze be humid. The climate change could only mean one thing. It had to be close.

Yuki's nose flared as her pupils narrowed into slits. Her skin started to ridge, protection from the unknown. In the presense of her own kind she didn't take any chances. Usually all battles that were fought on Terra were to be in human form, but with this creature it was from her world, uninvited,and from the 7th dimension where all exist.

Sensei was right behind Yuki as they stood back to back scanning their surroundings in a circular motion. He was the oldest living being alive on Terra. His frame, lean but sturdy with multiple muscles bulging, almost always compared to the legendary Bruce Lee. The life expectancy averaged between 200 to 300 years of age. Sensei was 215 but was agile as a teen-ager thanks to his gifts.

In his earlier years, Sensei used to be the head of the Fate Seekers. When he was in command it was both males and females. When his protege' Yuki took over, she changed the dynamics of the estate. A part of the cycle meant that after you lead, you must teach. Now he was the teacher of the Dojo. All the students came through him to pass an extensive line of training to become a Fate Seeker. This was his only obligation until the portal was opened and a couple of lost souls from the Fate Lands escaped.

Replica ordered for Sensei to assist Yuki in the speedy capture or killing of the bandits. It was to be done as quietly as possible to maintain balance in this dimension, Terra, the third dimension.

Rock Creek Park, it was a deeply wooded area that by law closed after dark. It is Federal grounds, no trespassing or loitering, prosecution guaranteed. The silence was deafening as both Yuki and Sensei desperately tried to find the creature.

The voice was demonic. "Ha ha haaaaahhh!"

It was close so close but so far away. Yuki took a few steps forward separating the closeness of her to Sensei. A heated draft whisked him. In lightening speed, he spun around to the humidity that brushed his back and swung his sword.

Nothing.

Nobody.

Yuki looked to the sky after hearing her eagle make a sound. It was flying in place, soaring nowhere. It was pinpointing the creatures location. "There!" Yuki pointed.

She ran, Sensei was on her heels as both were on a full out sprint. Snow began to fall. Big fluffy flakes smacked their faces as they came to a sliding halt.

This is it!

The thorn that was in Yuki's back that cost so many lives months ago. Ethan McDonald, no longer was it considered a person, it was nothing but a lost soul of the afterlife of the Fate Lands.

Instead of his once 6 foot frame, Ethan now stood 12 feet with a lanky deteriorated corpse of his once human body. Observing his frame, it appeared stretched out with each movement. As It moved, the skin tore, exposing ripped tendons and opened sores.

It smiled in their presence. "Konichiwa, Yuki. We meet again or should I say sayonara, HA HA HA HAH-HH!." Ethan enjoyed a belly laugh.

Sensei turned to Yuki, "You know this thing?"

"Remember Hawaii?" Sensei nodded but never broke his visual of the creature as Yuki continued. "Well, that's the afterlife version."

Sensei shook his head and took his fighting stance. "What is it?" Yuki smiled than sang, "Tah dah, " Her arms wide spread as if she was presenting Ethan as a gift. "One of the Fate lands creations." Then quickly got in her survival stance as well.

Ethan swung a punch at Yuki who in turn ducked and summersaulted out of the way. Ethan's punch connected with a big mahogany tree that splintered after his arm forcefully went through it.

Birds flew as small rodents jumped to the nearest tree for sanctuary, abandoning their now fallen habitat. Sensei was airborne. As the tree was falling, Sensei was on the attack. He swung his sword, a stainless steel forged in fire blade, at the torso of Ethan, slicing through his flesh like butter as he landed with a bloody sword.

No sooner than Sensei landed like a leaf, Yuki countered his attack. She delivered a mean combination of furious blows to the abdomen and face of a now kneeling Ethan who in turn was holding his stomach that threatened to come out, a piece of the exit wounds from the potentially fatal attack from Sensei.

Ethan groaned. He was wounded, but not defeated. One hand on the ground, he inhaled some dirt. This action confused Yuki but not Sensei who screamed. "Nooooo! We have to finish him."

It was too late, the dirt was his energy reboot. Whereas Yuki and The Fate Seekers would use the pond to strengthen all gifts which held the Fate Lands mystical waters.

Ethan being a dead soul of The Fate Lands, he could use the dirt from Terra or any other world to regain his strengths. The Fate Lands underworld was his new forever home.

The snow started to stick, covering the ground rapidly. This was good for Yuki. An edge The advantage. With the ground covered he couldn't regain any energy.

Ethan stood tall. Oblivious to the snow painting the ground. In his demonic voice he taunted. "Is that all you got!"

Yuki and Sensei made eye contact, silently communicating through facial expressions and body language. Sensei nodded to the ground. Yuki smiled, knowing what he was implying. It was the same thing that she noticed.

The snow.

It was coming down with a vengeance. They ran in hopes that Ethan would give chase. Their high speed sprint could reach speeds of 60mph and that was the speed they were now running at.

"DONT RUN NOW!" Ethan gave chase.

His stride looked like he was gliding. His long frame helped him get closer with each step. Slipping a couple times, he regained his traction. Running full speed, he came to a sliding halt. As he stopped, his eyes widened.

Ethan knew it was too late, even though he was yet to be touched.

Silence.

Ethan looked around. He couldn't see anything.

He sniffed.

The aroma was potent. They were around here some-where. A sound. He spotted them high. Ethan looked and he narrowed his eyes for confirmation.

No.

Birds.

The sounds of feathers flapping rapidly as if some-thing spooked the swarm away. Heavy snow fell off the branches hitting Ethan on his head as he brushed his face, clearing his vision. Sensei came high. Yuki came low. Sensei from the right, Yuki from the left. Sensei was in the air, both hands on his ancient sword raised to the sky, ready to come down on Ethan.

Yuki ahead of Sensei in the assault already swinging a big branch sweeping Ethan's legs from under him. Sensei on the descent turned his blade down as he landed on the upper torso of Ethan piercing his chest, then sliding the sword in a downward motion opening his insides.

"Ahhhh!" Ethan yelled in agony, tossing Sensei off his body with a sling of his arm.

Dropping the branch, Yuki reached for her ponytail now brandishing two of her custom made chopsticks designed to hold her hair but in all actuality were dag-gers. Rushing, trying to finish the job, Yuki was on the attack. Puncturing his abdomen with multiple quick strikes of the dagger, Ethan grew weak.

With his last bit of strength, he managed to ball up his hand creating a massive fist. He swung it connecting with Yuki's face sending her flying across the wooded park landing on an oncoming Sensei who recently got up from his attack.

Frantically, Ethan started to remove the snow in an attempt to regain his energy, but the dirt was now mud. He had no way of rejuvenation. Sensei and Yuki noticed him trying to regenerate and went on the attack, but to their surprise Ethan smiled then spoke as they neared.

"You might have won this round...Ha ha ha, " Then turned into dust in the air as they slid through his remains.

Sensei spoke, "We need to go to the Fate Lands."

Yuki frowned, she really wasn't trying to go and face Replica in fear of what he might know or suspect. "Why?"

"We need to get a weapon, the soul catcher. This Ethan creature has evolved and have the ability to float with the wind. This weapon would be able to take him back for good."

"I don't know why we just cant kill him, again that is. But if you want to capture him, lets head to the estate.

...Solo ignored Sarang's pleads. Sour taste and thoughts flooded his mind as he began to push through the crowded dance floor, aggressively. Ebony tried to pull her date in the opposite direction to avoid confrontation as Solo approached. Onyx and Teddy were his heels following him trying to catch up as the crowd seemed to part like the Red Sea.

The music was loud as the bass vibrated the floors. In Solo's mind it was complete silence, nothing but the sound of the wind as he briskly whisked past the oblivious partygoers making his way to his victim.

Emotions were mixed. This clouded his vision and the bigger picture, the task at hand became personal. Teddy caught up to Solo first and reached for his arm but grabbed his wrist instead, in an attempt to stop him.

"What the fuck!?" Teddy noticed the size of Solo's fist.

Solo snatched away still in pursuit. Teddy stopped dead in his tracks with wide eyes then looked inside the cup in his hand. Onyx ran into Teddy when he abruptly stopped.

"Whoa, what you just stop for? Grab him before he reach Ebony and Ol' Boy!"

"Fuck dat! Did you see the size of his fist," Teddy asked bubbled eyed. He looked at his cup again, "something aint right, Bro. I think somebody Bill Cosby'd me."

"What!? Man move!" Onyx brushed past Teddy following Solo to the back of the club.

Teddy followed, but as he did he looked in his cup one final time before tossing the rest of its contents on the floor.

"Uh Uh, not tonight, Bill."

CHAPTER 25

Sarang noticed the scene and thought it would go bad real fast if she didn't intervene. The lights inside the club flickered. It made it seem as if the patrons were shadows appearing and disappearing in still frame right before your eyes. She used this to her advantage by putting her gifts in motion.

Ascending high toward the ceiling she leaped across the dance floor landing directly behind Teddy.

"Whoa, what da fuck?" He turned around when he felt the cool draft on his neck.

Sarang quickly moved to his front side just as swiftly when Teddy turned around to see nothing behind him. When Teddy faced forward the only thing in his eyesight was Sarang's fist approaching his throat at a rapid speed knocking him out instantly.

Before he could fall on the sticky floor, Sarang was behind him catching his body. With her arms under his armpits, she dragged him to a nearby couch that rested along side the wall. Quickly scanning the area, Sarang saw Onyx making his way to the back room. That was what she was trying to avoid. If Onyx saw Solo in that state of mind, it could be bad for his health, especially if Yuki was to find out.

Sarang jumped and glided across the floor landing in front of a random guy dancing. He opened his eyes with surprise. "Hey, Sweetness! Da hell you come from?" He danced as he spoke. Sarang smiled then walked through the double doors ignoring his passes...

"Who the hell is this, Ebony?" Solo asked as Ebony stood in the front of the mark like a shield when Solo began his approach.

"Solo Stop! It's not like that. He's just a friend from school that--"

"Oh! I'm just a friend now?" The mark interjected and side stepped. Solo grew irritated with his voice quickly. "Shut up, Homes! Aint nobody talkin' to you, Champ!" Solo was heated as he stepped toward the mark. Onyx grabbed his arm pulling him back.

"Chill, Cuz', she aint even worth it. She aint shit. I been telling you that. Lets just get up outta' here."

Ebony smacked her teeth, she didn't like his comments, "Fuck you, Onyx!"

her date grabbed her arm, "Come on, Boo, forget them lames."

"WHAT YOU SAY!" Solo snatched away from Onyx's grip. Sarang came through the doors as her senses heightened. She ran fast as time seemed to slow down. First hitting Onyx with the exact move that put Teddy to sleep as he turned around to the opening door. Before Onyx's body crashed on the floor, Sarang stood directly in front of Solo with her palms on his stomach holding him back. Her backside faced Ebony as she looked into Solo's eyes.

"Breathe." She told him imitating breathing techniques.

Ebony stepped forward. "And who da hell is dis' bitch?"

Sarang looked over her shoulder, smiled but didn't respond. Instead she made a quick move placing her directly in front of ebony connecting a punch sending her through a table where she landed unconscious.

"Finish it, Solo," Sarang said leaving out but not before saying, "and meet me out front."

Solo narrowed his eyes at the sight of his mark. He never got his name. Really it didn't matter. In his eyes the guy was a dead man walking. What at first was only a calling, quickly turned into a vendetta. He only wished he had more time and a better location to really make him hurt.

The guy was panicked, especially after he saw his girl-friend fly through a table that was a clear fifteen feet away. The look in his Solo's eyes had him nervous and scared in the same moment after his pupils turned demonic red and his fist swelled the size of boxing gloves.

"Listen, Man, you could h-have her. She aint even w-worth us beefin', Fam."

"First of all, we aint fam', as you put it. secondly this thing is way bigger than me and you."

He looked confused. "What you mean!?"

Solo smiled mischievously. "What i mean is if Ebony was out here being a slut or not, this was still the last chapter in your book. Fate has called your number," He walked closer with each word and continued, "All you did by fucking with her was make it that much more sweeter for me."

"Man I don't know what the hell you talking about. All i know is that I'm not doing to make it easy." He said putting his hands up in a fighting stance.

The mark was a big guy and about ten to fifteen pounds heavier. Solo smiled at the gesture. "Wouldn't have it any other way." he put his defense stance in place.

The big guy swung!

It was a wild haymaker that Solo dodged and re-turned with a hook of his own that connected with his chin bringing the mark down to a knee. Solo held back his strength purposefully.

The guy from one knee spit out a tooth that rested on his tongue and eyed Solo with a grim expression. in return, Sol smiled. "Make your next move your best move."

The guy stood up and ran at Solo who in turn kneeled as he built the strength and released an uppercut that sent the mark in the air, his head going through the ceiling leaving only his feet dangling with residue falling.

Solo pulled him front the hole letting him fall to the floor with a concussion. The guy was delirious. Solo bent over behind him placing a sleeper hold that ended his life when he exhaled his last breath.

Solo looked around to see Onyx still passed out along with Ebony under the table still snoring. he scratched his head. "Where's Teddy!?" He walked to Onyx and was about to shake him but decided against it. Waking him would mean explaining what happened and that wasn't an option.

He walked back through the set of double doors where the music was loud and the lights flickered. He eased through the crowd in search of the exit. The calling was complete.

Sarang paced the sidewalk waiting for Solo to complete her calling. Her mind was conflicted. So much had been going on in her world that she didn't understand. Why was she feeling any type of way about Solo? She couldn't determined her exact emotion. Was it anger? Annoyance? Jealously? 'OF COURSE NOT!' Sarang shook off the last thought.

No way could she be jealous of the way Solo acted over some girl. His girl? Sarang saw Solo looking for her and kneeled behind a parked car. She didn't want to be seen right then. Slowly she backpedaled passing each car and disappeared with the night lights.

Solo sighed heavily after not being able to locate Sarang. His breathing leveled out after a short while as his fist shrank. he smiled looking at his fist. Standing at the door thoughts of his friends surfaced. Since he wasn't able to find Sarang, he re-entered the club. He couldn't just leave his friends anyway.

The DJ was spinning the latest tracks as Solo's shoulder automatically started to bounce to the beat as he made his way through the club. The first person he located was Teddy passed out on a love seat.

"Aye, Fat Boy! Get up." Solo began to shake him. Teddy eye's began to open, "Stay right here. I'm about to go get Onyx then we outta here." Teddy blinked multiple times not really understanding what was being told to him but agreed.

Solo continued to sway through the crowd with multiple woman trying to grab his attention to which he just smiled and kept heading toward the back where Onyx rested. Going through the double doors, Onyx was slowly standing up making it to his feet.

Before he could get completely aware, Solo wrapped his arms around him spinning him to the door in attempt to blind him from both of the bodies that laid across the room. One dead, the other unconscious. "Hey Big Boy, you ite?" Solo guided him through the door. "I don't know what the hell you and Teddy been drinking but ya'll was trippin' and passed out," Onyx was looking around confused rubbing his neck as Solo continued, "We gotta go get Teddy so we can roll, you hear me?"

Onyx didn't verbally respond. He only nodded swallowing dry spit. Walking through the crowd of people, the lights flickered and the bass vibrated the floor which made Onyx's head pound more.

Teddy was in the same spot with his head in his own lap when Solo tapped his shoulder. "Lets go, Homie!" Teddy was groggy but stood up.

"What happened?"

Solo shook his head, "Somebody gave ya'll something. You started seeing shit then passed out."

He began to rub his head trying to recall past events. "All I remember is seeing you 'bout to beat up some dude...oh yeah! Your fist was big as shit, no bullshit, like the fuckin' Hulk!"

"See what I mean, time to go."

"Nah for real, you was like Incredible Nigga!"

"Man shut up and lets get up outta here."

Exiting the club, Solo and his friends headed to the car and pulled off in the nights air not even noticing

Sarang leaned on the wall blending in with the darkness of the night on the opposite side of the street.

CHAPTER 26

Sarang waited silently in the creases of the night. Patiently on alert. She knew what had to be done in the near future. Sirens became to vocalize the night air as they wailed.

First to arrive was the police, secondly was the paramedics. That's who she had been waiting for, the latter. Two bodies were gurnied out. One in a sheet, the other being rushed to the ambulance as the paramedics rushed to strap an oxygen mask over the victims mouth.

"Tst," Sarang smacked her teeth then blew a sigh. "You know better, solo, no witnesses," She mumbled turning on her heels headed for her car.

It was a Chevy Corvette Z51. It's v-8 engine with its zero to sixty in 2.8 seconds capability made it easy to narrow the distance between her and the ambulance as it headed to the hospital.

Pulling in the hospital's parking lot, she watched the paramedics rush Ebony through the emergency automatic double doors hurriedly. Sarang checked her surroundings and noticed a staff member heading to his car. He looked to be a doctor. Before he could open his door after unlocking it, Sarang was in front of him blocking his path. he jumped.

"Oh my! You scared me," The doctor held his chest. "How are you doing Miss? Need help with something?"

She smiled. "Actually I do."

In a quick motion she double tapped his groin area with four fingers forcing him to hunch over from the quick sensation, then quickly jabbed his throat demobilizing him as he fell into her arms.

She stripped him of his medical jacket and credentials then tossed him on his own backseat. Walking through the hospital with purpose, Sarang followed the signs and located the trauma center.

Ebony was stable as Sarang read her chart. Nurses walked by, some waved, others were in awe of the beauty of the accomplished doctor but kept comments to themselves. Peeking in the hallway, noticing it was clear, Sarang closed the door and pulled the curtain back.

Ebony was wide awake with bubbled eyes of recognition. "W-what're you doing here for?" She was visibly scared.

Sarang smiled. "I see you're alive and well. Guess Solo couldn't finish the job huh?"

"The job?!"

"Yes, kill you, duh."

"Kill me?" She tried to lean up.

"Yup, our employer my name of, Fate, don't like loose ends," Sarang shrugged reaching for a pillow. "but I'll make it quick, okay."

"HELP-"Ebony's screams were muffled by the pillow cutting her airwaves off eventually silencing her as she suffocated trying to fight. Sarang was too long as Ebony's kicks slowed with her inhaling her last breath. Sarang leaned in Ebony's ear and got close. "Ill take care of, Solo, now." She grinned and tossed the pillow exiting the room.

CHAPTER 27

As Sarang crept through the side doors of the hospital disappearing into the night, Yuki was getting out of the shower in preparation to enter The Otherworld on the other side of the black door. That was her one and only passage to the Fate Lands. Sensei sat in the tea room in a robe with his feet soaking in lemon water as the slices floated. He missed that feeling of relaxation and when his only duty was to direct his fate seekers in the right direction. The cycle of life changed which also changed his obligations.

Yuki came into the room with just a tower on as waster dripped off her hair and ran down the creases of her body.

"Diajobu?" Yuki asked if he was okay.

"Hai, fine." Sensei looked her way and smiled. Yuki had the look of confusion. She was wondering if he was "okay" then why wasn't he getting prepared to accompany her to the Fate Lands. Sensei read her thoughts and commented. " I'm not going with you. I don't have any words for replica, if he doesn't summon me I don't go, Ja Mata." He gave her a slight wave telling her, He'll see her later.

Yuki bowed. Warkarimashta." Slowly backing up informing that she understood.

Sensei smiled and nodded but not before saying, "Gambatte," Wishing her good luck.

Yuki turned on heels and headed for the Black door. Walking through the halls she passed a few seekers and they bowed their respects as she passed. Opening the door, a cool draft instantly placed chill bumps on her skin and made her nipples erect through the towel.

The Fate Lands creatures swam in the pond and walked around the room freely drifting from different dimensions. The room itself felt like another world as fog loomed in the air. As Yuki placed a foot in the pond-like pool letting the towel fall, her skin began to form ridges upon contact of the water.

The pheromones that the hairless six legged cats released began to seal all cuts and bruises from the fight against The Fate Lands Ethan. The deeper her body sank into the water, the faster she began to crystalize.

Its waters began to swirl rapidly as if a whirlwind was swallowing her body taking her on the exhausting trip to the Fate Lands.

From experience, during the trip through thru 7th dimension Yuki kept her eyes wide open. If she closed them the bright lights upon entry would blind her. Dropping from the sky, the air was cool but deceiving. The closer she fell to the ground the more humid it became.

Landing on the ground with her knees slightly bent and her hands beneath her flat on the ground, Confusion etched her face. Beneath her body was six inches of freezing snow that didn't melt in the hundred degree atmosphere.

The sun was the color of a ripe banana and made the air wavy with heat. Yuki looked around and the gates weren't flaming. They were bright red with black smoke rising off them.

She approached, already knowing what to expect. Yuki stopped at the entrance and put a hand on her hip. She looked around. "I know you're here! I don't have time for your games!" She yelled to the air.

Silence.

It lingered for two long minutes before the strong and heavy foot steps began to make the ground shake. The sound of the stomps seemed to be coming from everywhere and Yuki couldn't pin point its location as the raspy voice finally spoke.

"Welcome back, Slave. I see that you are by your lonesome, " he mad e himself visible. "I'm glad you didn't cross the gates. I would love to make you bleed." Deathtidus twirled a jagged sword around finally stopping in front of Yuki looking down on her.

"Yea, yea, you wish," Yuki waved him off. "I'm here for Replica, do I need an escort or are you going to let me through."

He grinned. "follow your path, Slave and hope your calling isn't near." Deathtidus side stepped.

Yuki narrowed her eyes at his grim expression as saliva left his lips along with blood from his last victim who past the gates without permission. She walked the dark path after lighting a torch gaining sights of four feet in front as only eyes peeked at her through the darkness.

The snow leveled out and became mud, then golden sand by the time she made it to the chambers where a empty throne sparkled. The closer Yuki steeped, the quicker the sand beneath her feet began to race in front of her forming a figure that sat on the throne.

Yuki stood before Replica and gave a slight bow but felt weird after she noticed Sarang being sculpted from the sand. replica smiled at Yuki with the face of Sarang then spoke.

"No, Solo?"

"Not yet, but he'll be here. I just have more pressing issues right now. It's Ethan, but before I tell you would you mind informing me why you took the form of her?"

Replica stood in Sarang's shapely figure. "This figure seems to weigh heavy on your mind, in short, I just let the mind create its appearance. Do you wish to talk about it?" He asked in her voice.

Yuki inhaled a sigh, "No, I rather not."

"You will...eventually."

"I'm here for Ethan. Somehow he has escaped and threatens to bring terror to Earth. I need access to the soul catcher before he goes through another portal and release more of his kind."

"Permission granted, anything else?"

"No, Master." Yuki turned to leave but was stopped with Replica's last words.

"Bring, Solo to me before you're unable."

Yuki turned around to respond just in time to see Replica turn into the dust he formed from. She wasn't sure exactly what the last comment meant, but had an idea. Replica was saying Solo could become a potential problem if unchecked.

Yuki began to walk the way she came with heavy thoughts. Replica wanted her to bring Solo, she wanted to deal with Ethan, but Sarang wanted answers from her. So much had to get accomplished. her decision was simple.

Simplicity.

Deal with the latter, which was Sarang. Making it to the gate, Deathtidus stood twirling a flaming sword with a grim expression. Multiple eyes lurked from the shadows blinking eagerly in anticipation of some type of action. Deathtidus didn't say a word, only stood blocking the exit. Yuki paused in her tracks. To her left was the exact same sword that Deathtidus wielded. his smile widened when he noticed Yuki looking at it.

She extended her hand about to grab it as she stared at him. She was tired of his idle threats. She knew she could take him. Yuki wrapped her fingers around the handle of the sword. Getting a solid grip, the blade of the sword flamed. Yuki clenched he jaw turning to face, Deathtidus, but changed her mind, releasing the sword as the flame disappeared.

Yuki inhaled a breath. "Excuse me, Deathtidus. May I exit, please?" She swallowed her pride and gave in to the gatekeeper.

He let out a belly laugh and moved to the side. "Sure you can. Remember who you are...a slave, now leave!" he demanded.

Yuki walked past the gate where a holographic tunnel shot straight from the ground to the sky with a continuous upward pulse. She stopped in front of it and glanced back at Deathtidus. "We'll have our day." Then jumped in the tunnel that ascended her through the dimensions back to the mansion.

Exiting the pond-like pool she walked as her skin turned from scaly to smooth in a matter of seconds. Grabbing a robe and swinging it around her shoulders, she reached for the doorknob and exited the room.

The scene went from black to bright white as the lights shined from the hallway. Yuki made her way to the tea room where sensei sat in deep meditation but finished up when he felt her presence.

He looked toward her. "How did it go?"

"Good I guess, and we have permission to go retrieve the soul catcher and pursue Ethan but I have another pressing issue right now."

Sensei smiled. "Sarang."

Yuki narrowed her eyes wondering who he knew. he caught the look. 'remember I raised you, then her. It's my job to know what you're thinking." He said then closed his eyes going back to his meditation ritual.

Yuki closed the door and headed for the room to get dresses. grabbing her phone she sent a text:

(NEED TO C U)

The receiver of the text was Sarang.

CHAPTER 28

Riley tiptoed out of Solo's room as he slept. The night before was very eventful and rest was needed to digest his endeavors. Riley was steadily preparing his daily mischief of the day. It was clockwork. So repetitive that it was to the point their mother didn't believe Solo would fall for suck trickery.

Valerie was in the kitchen making breakfast which put the aroma of crispy bacon in the air. The smell had Solo tossing and turning in his sleep threatening to wake up.

Riley had to hurry.

His plan was coming together. He rubbed his hands together and balled his face up at the thought of Solo. The previous night when Solo made it home from the nightclub, he first headed to his mother's room and placed a kiss on her forehead as she slept. Walking softly he then headed to Riley's room.

Riley was asleep.

He slept comfortably curled up in a ball with one arm between his thighs and a thumb in his mouth. Solo smirked and headed for the kitchen. In there, the smirk he wore became a wide grin as he mixed hot sauce, vinegar and mayo in a spoon then headed back to Riley's room.

Solo walked softly and stood over Riley. In a quick motion he snatched Riley's thumb out his mouth and coated it with the special sauce he just invented. Literally on his toes, he crept out the room as Riley rolled over placing his thumb back into his mouth. Solo ran down the hall and closed his bedroom door and went to sleep with a smile on his face after hearing the wails of Riley...

Riley finished the last few touches of his set up with revenge on his mind. Solo yawned and stretched when his eyes began to open. Leaning up in his bed he looked around trying to gather his thoughts and remember where he was.

The night before was crazy to say the least. All he hoped was that the deceptional story he told his friends would hold and they wouldn't question him. Yuki would have their heads if she found out Teddy and Onyx knew or remembered anything.

The Fate seekers covenant lasted centuries by keeping its secret a secret. His other thoughts revolved around Ebony. Thinking of her, he instantly jumped out his bed heading for the dresser that sat on the opposite side of the room.

Once both feet were placed on the floor, he dashed for the phone, but lost his footing as he slipped on his own bowl of marbles that were spread on his floor.

"Whoa!," His feet shot straight to the ceiling. he landed hard on the newly laid text tile floor panels. "A-ahh, shit! my back," He moaned as he crawled to his knees then his feet and whispered. "Ok, Riley, it's on."

Solo walked to the door cautiously and opened it, but quickly jumped to the side not knowing what to expect. It was clear. To make sure he waved his foot through the clearing trying to trigger any hidden tricks or camouflage traps.

Nothing.

Leaving his room, Solo went straight to Riley's room and opened the door. Riley was asleep in the bed still in pajamas from the night before. Solo just knew Riley hadn't been out of the bed yet. He smiled as he crept to the sleeping riley. The closer he came, the wider the grin on his face became.

Little did he know, Riley was staring at him through the sheer sheets with squinted eyes and his own grin plastered on his face. Solo was so excited to catch his brother in such a vulnerable state that he missed the thin thread of floss that lined the floor that he walked through which triggered enough power to tilt over a 7-eleven Big Gulp cup filled with glitter and baby oil.

"What the f-!" Solo tensed up in shock as the liquid ran down his face and back, "Ima kill you!!" He dived on the bed trying to grab Riley who rolled to the opposite side of the bed landing on the floor where he began to crawl, then jumped up running out the room. Solo was in pursuit as he came off the same side as Riley and ran after him but was slowed up as a strip of invisible plastic's wrap covered his face forcing him to trip as he tried to unbind his face.

Riley peeked around the hallway into the room to see Solo just beginning to stand up. Riley licked his tongue and put his thumbs in his ears with his free fingers waving.

"Na-na-nah-boo-boo!" He sang then ran down the hallway to a flight of stairs.

By the time Solo made it down the stairs, Valerie was at the bottom. "Stop running in my damn house," She paused and got a good look at her eldest son, "boy, what kind of freaky stuff you into...coming down the stairs all shiny and shit? Is it something you want to tell me?" She placed a hand on her hip.

"Huh?! What are you talkin' about, Ma?"

"Nevermind but did you see the news?" She asked.

Solo balled his fist up looking at Riley at the dinner table about to eat still licking his tongue behind their mother's back but answered. "No, Ma. I don't watch the news, aint nuthin' good ever come from it."

"well you better start. Your little girlfriend that supposed to be in school died in the hospital last night.

the news saying the doctors don't seem to know what happened. She was stable, then dead. God work in mysterious ways, Child, I tell you." Valerie said and headed to the kitchen.

Solo frowned his face and mumbled. "That wasn't the work of no God." He followed his mother to the kitchen where he sat on the opposite side of Riley.

Riley smiled. "Hey, Big Bro! I miss you."

Valerie smiled at them as Solo narrowed his eyes. "Whateva', Punk pass the grits."

CHAPTER 29

Sarang tossed and turned all night. Sleep didnt come easy. Thoughts of her whole existence loomed in the air. What to do? How to react? Hate it or love it? As she drove, Sarang occasionally looked at her opened phone that revealed a text from Yuki that she has yet to reply to.

The message requested , no demanded, that she comes to her. Sarang didn't feel like the obedient daughter she used to be. Just a week ago she would've dropped everything to find out what Yuki wanted or needed.

Today was the lesser, today she could care less. Really she wanted to call and check on Solo, but why? She never wanted or cared about his well being before.

'HE MIGHT BE MAD AT ME IF HE FOUND OUT ABOUT HIS LITTLE GIRLFRIEND' Sarang thought as she tossed her phone on the seat.

She felt like she was off her game and only Yuki could tell her why. Only Yuki could see into her eyes like open doors. the mansion was where she was headed. the drive to the estate was on the other side of the city. She arrived in twenty five minutes and slowly cruised the driveway leading to the entrance.

Sarang's temperature was high, emotionally hot, as she slammed the car door and walked up the stairs. A maid stood at the top of the stairs and cheerfully spoke.

"Ohayou Gozaimas!" good morning she greeted.

Sarang narrowed her eyes and flipped the maid the 'bird'. "The fuck it is!" Then walked through the wide spread double doors.

the maid followed her in. "Ma'am! Ma'am!," She called to Sarang as she walked behind her, "your shoes, Ma'am."

Entering the mansion, the rules are etched in stone. Always take your shoes off at the door and replace them with a pair of slips. Once again Sarang gave the maid her finger to kiss and continued to walk. She headed for the spiral staircase in search of Yuki. No one dared block her path.

On the inside she wanted to leave. Sarang felt Yuki's presence as it lingered all over and didn't seem to leave her alone. The wounds to the heart that she didn't know she had didn't seem like they could heal.

The more she thought of the betrayal the angrier she became. She made it to the top foyer of the estate and headed to the room she suspected Yuki would be.

Walking down the hall, she passed the Black door as a cool breeze blew from underneath the door. the aroma was alluring and slowed her stride. Slowly she passed, temptation almost stopped her but the anger felt for Yuki kept her feet moving.

Sarang stopped at a door, without knocking she entered and stood with her arms folded silently. Yuki's back was turned as she spoke, "Do you think Ill ever need you, love you, more than you'll need me?" Sarang tapped her foot rapidly with no comment as Yuki continued. "I sense there's some things on your mind. Don't keep them to yourself, express yourself." Yuki stated calmly sitting crossed legged. Her back still toward Sarang.

"Who am I?" Sarang returned her calm.

"Sarang, daughter of Yuki, anything else?"

Sarang quickly became irate. "No I'm not! Really, who was I before you stole me?"

"Doesn't matter."

Sarang tilted her head. "And my mother is where?"

"Dead."

"You killed her?"

"For the greater good." Yuki replied still in her meditation stance. The only muscle she used was her mouth when she spoke.

Yuki responses were dry. It had Sarang livid as Yuki continued. "Listen, Love," She said calling Sarang by the definition of her name. "I thought we were great, but it feels like you're taking your love back. You standing there missing what you never had. I'm assuming Solo is bringing some feelings out of you that you wish to explore. That is forbidden. there is no place for that. I will kill your precious Solo to ensure you stay on task. I will also-"

"Nooo!" Sarang ran toward Yuki who didn't flinch or move as four fate seekers descended from the ceiling landing in front of Sarang.

Sarang punched the first one that attempted to grab her. The power behind the assault made the seeker fly to the back wall as her eyes became slits. The next came and ran into a round house kick knocking her back into the other two. Yuki finally stood and raised her hand. "Enough!"

Everyone stopped abruptly . Sarang heaved ready to continue the fight. Yuki turned to Sarang. "Get out! Don't come back until you calm yourself...but remember all I've said, now leave!"

Yuki turned her back before Sarang could respond.

The four fate seekers stood guard as Sarang turned to the door making her exit. She still didn't have complete answers. Her temper interrupted her thoughts and questions. What she did know was that she wasn't going to let Yuki harm Solo.

Whatever she was feeling for him trumped the feelings she once had for Yuki. Inside the car she sat for five minutes before even turning the ignition over in the vehicle. She sent Solo a text to which he didn't reply. Tired of waiting, she finally put the car in gear and pulled off.

To reliever the stress Sarang decided and made the Dojo her destination. She figured it to be the place to blow some steam and maybe get some better answers from Sensei.

Traffic was slow. There was an accident f ew blocks away and commuters weren't able to detour through the residential area. Violations carried heavy fines and hassles of being pulled over by the local law enforcement for a longer time than one would've waited in traffic for. Knowing the outcome, she inched on for a quarter mile before the flow of traffic became normal. Parking in front of the Dojo, Sarang climbed the stairs to the entrance. The door was ajar. Pushing through, it creaked wider as she crossed the threshold where a draft of wind passed that was so strong it forced her to step back and regain her balance.

Walking through the halls, she headed for the main Dojo where she heard the grunts of a fighter punching a bag or somebody. The closer she came the clearer the grunts were understood as words. She listened.

"Fuck! Her!," Two jabs hit the bag. "She, aint, shit, anyway!"

The combination of kicks and punches landed with anger behind each blow. Sarang turned the corner to see Solo dripping in sweat wearing nothing but shorts. Instinctively she touched herself when a tingle came. She ignored the foreign feeling.

"Ahem!," Sarang grabbed Solo's attention. "I hope you wasn't talking about me." She leaned on the wall and crossed her arms.

Solo grabbed the towel and wiped his face of the sweat that leaked off his face and chest. "Listen, Xenia Warrior Princess. It's a lot of bullshit goin' on. It's all bad, it's all real but to answer your question, no, I wasn't talkin' about you," he narrowed his eyes. "Even though I saw the news. It had to be done. I knew you would do it anyways."

"Well it looks like you came here for the same reasons I did. One being to relieve some stress. Soooo, you want to spar?"

Solo laughed. "spar? You think you ready?" He rubbed his hands together. "this aint like when we first met. I'll beat yo' ass now."

Sarang walked toward Solo. "Is that right?"

"Damn straight! I use to think it was sexist to hit a woman until I realized it was sexist not to hit a woman, right? Equal treatment means equal ass whoopin's for all, so come get you some!"

Sarang paused for a slight second. "Where's Sensei?"

"He aint here, cant nobody save you, just you and me here, Sweetness, so what's up?" Solo taunted. "Ready to get dis' ass whoopin'?"

Sarang smiled. In the same second, she attacked with a flying kick with her leg extended and the other bent at the knee. Solo eye's widened at the quick move but wasn't quick enough to block the assault as it connected sending him to the wall.

By the time his back hit the wall, Sarang was there delivering a two punch combo' that stopped Solo from sliding down the wall. The third punch came as Solo grabbed her fist before it connected and twisted it turning her body around. Her back was to his chest as he finessed a sleeper hold on her.

"Go to sleep, go to sleeeep..." He squeezed.

Sarang elbowed him forcing him to loosen his grip as she turned around with a roundhouse punch that connected solidly with his chin sending him across the opposite side of the Dojo landing through a table that held different weapons.

Sitting in the middle of the broken table, Solo leaned up on his arms. "Oh, it's like dat'?" He jumped to his feet. "you still punch like a girl, anyway!" Solo said in an attempt to anger her.

Sarang hated to be compared to an earthling, but with the new found information it pulled a different feeling and Solo noticed her facial expression but it confused him.

"Hey, You ite?"

Sarang blinked quickly pushing thoughts of Yuki out her mind. "Worry about yourself, not me!" She screamed and ran toward Solo full speed in attempt to tackle him.

The attack was reversed when Solo wrapped his arms around her body flipping her on her back with him landing on top. They locked eyes. Solo grinned. "What you think about-"

Sarang leaned up and kissed Solo on his lips silencing him. She broke the kiss and laid flat on the floor staring at Solo. He tilted his head to side then shrugged leaning forward and kissed Sarang.

The kiss was passionate as they began to let their hands roam freely along each others bodies. Sarang was in paradise and her body began to react to his touch as Solo expertly undid the bow of her sweatpants. She easily and willingly wiggled out of them. Still kissing, Solo ran his hands under her boy short panties to feel the moistness of her clitoris.

He broke the kiss and pulled his finger out, "Damn,- Girl, you wet as shit!"

Sarang was breathing heavy, "W-wet?! Is t-that good?"

Solo grinned. "Damn sure is, let me show you."

Solo licked her neck, down to her stomach then the jungle of her pubic hairs that she never shaved. It looked like slime as Sarang kept climaxing from his touch. Solo placed a fat, warm tongue on her love button causing her to shake from the foreign feeling.

Instinctively, she punched Solo who rolled off her after the sucker punch connected. He rubbed his jaw and smiled as he noticed Sarang still flat on her back with her legs cocked wide. he dived right back in and licked her making circles around her silky hairs and rapidly rotated his tongue in and out of her juicebox that leaked like a faucet coating his face with gloss.

Sarang rolled her eyes in ecstacy. She was on cloud nine making her the highest in the room. Solo was ready. he was so brick that his tool began to hurt trying to fight out his pants.

As he licked, he slid his pants off and his manhood sprung out like a jack in the box. he kissed her stomach and eased up her body back to her mouth as she greedily accepted his tongue. Slowly he lined himself to her cherry center and entered. Sarang eyes widened. A soft exotic moan left her in a sigh. She dug her nails deep into Solo's back as her mouth opened in a 'O' shape of pleasure.

Solo kept a slow pace as he body started to accept his girth of pain for pleasure. When he felt her thrusting toward him he lifted himself to his knees and flipped her around never pulling out and began to pound as he wrapped her hair in a ball around his hand.

The thigh to cheek sound along with the visual waves of Sarang butterscotch butt had Solo going crazy. The sexual moans coming from Sarang was the endgame as he couldn't hold his eruption anymore. He exploded inside Sarang and they both collapsed drenched in sweat. All that could be heard was heavy breathing. After about five minutes of silence Sarang popped up out of nowhere.

"Yuki gonna kill you!"

Solo looked over from his back, "Wait, what?!"

CHAPTER 30

THE MANSION

"I heard some commotion, I take it was your daughter." Sensei said entering the room.

"Hmph, some daughter. You should have seen how she reacted when I told her my plans for Solo. The little demon child tried to attack me!"

Sensei chuckled, "Attack you?" Yuki nodded as he continued. "You know we will never understand the human emotion of love. It's your fault she is rebelling. You've waited too long to tell her." Sensei coughed then continued in his raspy voice. "You created this new hatred in her heart and might have let her internal beast out the cage." Sensei sat with his cup of tea as Yuki stood from meditation.

"A beast? Ha! She may be mad but she's not stupid. She'll get over it. Enough about her, we have a bigger problem at hand. We need to track Ethan and return his soul back to the Fate Lands before he unleash chaos on Terra.

Sensei waved his hand nonchalantly. "he will get dealt with. You need to be worried about that firecracker you sent out of here. " He raised his hands in surrender, "but you're The Head of the snake so I'll follow your lead." he bowed with a bit of sarcasm attacked to it.

Yuki smiled and licked her lips. "it's time to take a trip to the archives."

"The archives, what you know about the archives?"

"Not much but what I do know is that that's where the soul catcher located."

The Archives was hidden in plain sight inside the Smithsonian. Every few generations its location is moved to stay hidden and blended in with the times or era.

Leaving the estate they were headed for downtown DC. It was a high traffic area where vigilance was a must when traveling to enter a secret cavern inside a high tourist attraction. During the drive a plan was discussed.

Entering the Smithsonian was no charge. There were tourist guides you could pay to help or you had the choice to roam by your lonesome.

Yuki and Sensei chose the latter.

Being of Asian ethnicity, they both looked like tourist which made it easier to blend. The hard part was was getting past the security guard that stood at the velvet rope entrance that was needed to get past.

Sensei stopped walking to observe a display label when Yuki stopped right beside him. "So what's next? Do we just walk to him and knock him out or just get him to move."

Sensei smiled and replied in a raspy voice. "I like the first idea but maybe that'll draw too much attention. We need a distraction."

"I'll get his attention long enough for you to go in and I wont be far behind, ok."

"What are you going to do?"

"Get it done," She clenched her jaw, "now stay by the big lizard exhibit." Yuki said referring to the T-Rex that had a group of school kids surrounding it.

Noticing the children, Yuki came up with an idea for the distraction needed to get her and Sensei clear. Walking toward Sensei she told him to go on the other side while she talked to the kids.

He shrugged his shoulders and complied. Yuki put a friendly smile on her face and spoke. "Hey children!" he voice a little higher than she expected.

There were Two boys and one girl, all in school uniforms on what she assumed was a school trip. The little girl stepped forward with defiance and a hand on her non-existent hip. "What you want, Mama'san?" Her name was Zionna and she was confident. "chicken fried rice, salt pepper ketchup!" they started laughing all except the youngest kid. He actually became annoyed.

"Ya'll need to shut up! That's why we don't get to go nowhere now, always messing wit people, "he looked at Yuki. "sorry for my sister and cousin, Are you okay?" Lil Ced asked.

Yuki smiled at his manners. his innocents reminded her of Sarang when she was about his age which was about ten or eleven years old. "Yes I'm fine young man, actually I was wondering could you ask the security to come over and help you read the sign-"

Zionna stepped in front of her younger brother, "See, you being all nice to her and she think you cant even read."

"I'll pay you."

Yuki redirected.

The older boy stepped up in front of the both of them to face Yuki. "Pay us you mean, we're all together." CJ said.

Yuki smiled. "Sure, I'll pay all of you. how is a hundred dollars." She pulled the freshy printed bill from her bag and their eyes widened.

"SOLD!!!" Zionna snatched the money and began her act instantly screaming, "Excuse me! Excuse me, Mister. Can you come here, it's inpor'nt!"

The guard turned like he didn't hear the high pitched youth which caused all the kids to scream in unison. He turned quickly and headed their way as Yuki walked past him and jumped over the velvet rope and entered the restricted area of the museum.

It was silent as Yuki and Sensei waked the corridor. the only sound that could be heard was the soft hum of the elevator music that played throughout the building. Yuki caught up to Sensei and led the way. The last time she was here actually was when the building was under construction. Replica foresaw the longevity of the building and decided it would be the soul catchers home.

Stopping in the middle of the lightly dimmed hall she smiled. "It's here."

Sensei looked at the rock-like wall and stared for a while before turning his attention to Yuki. "Uhhh sooo, are you going to go get it or what?? His voice dry and raspy.

Yuki stepped forward to examine the wall as her eyes narrowed turning into snake-like slits. Scanning the wall she found what she was looking for and pressed the thumbnail sized rock which sank into the wall as a door began to form. becoming visible was a dark passageway full of dust and spiderwebs.

"Shall we?" Yuki gestured toward the entrance and Sensei headed in.

Once the both of them entered, the door closed and locked itself. "No turning back now, huh?" Yuki smiled. he didn't respond, only kept his stride and headed down the path.

When sensei was the Head of the Fate Seekers he never had to summon the help of the soul catcher. even though the situation was all bad, he was excited for the chance to see the ancient weapon put to work.

The cavern was full of mystic creatures scurrying about. the presence of two beings had the different species of all colors and sizes disperse into the crevices of any open cracks or spaces available. The Fate Lands creatures had no bones or skin. a creature the size of a cat could run and squeeze through any crease accessible.

The rapid movement encouraged Yuki to pick up her pace to close the distance between her and Sensei. She never likes the creatures even though they came from her own world. they were ugly and disfigured compared to Earth's creatures and creeped her out.

She was about to drift past Sensei when he put his hand out abruptly stopping her in her own tracks.

"Slow down...did you forget your lessons on the caverns. They are not as they seem."

Yuki's facial expressed instant remembrance as her eyes bubbled. Years ago when she was in training as a junior seeker, the entire class was taught about the soul catcher along with the dangers throughout the path in retrieving it.

A flood of memories rushed her mind and froze her in her tracks.

"You're right, what was I thinking?" She narrowed her eyes. "right there, toss something over that crossing." She pointed ahead.

"Good job, you remembered." Sensei grabbed a star from his waistline and flung it forward. After he released it, it soared spinning forward and was cut in half as a path sized a slammed in front of them blocking the path. Sensei looked at Yuki then gave a rare smile.

"Pay attention, it's a few more surprises if I remember correctly."

The ax started to rise slowly. they both cleared it before it reached the top to reset its sensors. "Yea I'm sure it is." Yuki said taking the lead.

Further and further they walked as the narrower the path became. She took a step and the silence in the air made the click sound deafening. "Shit!" Yuki paused.

"Yea, shit, back up!!" Sensei yelled pulling Yuki back.

In the nick of time Sensei was able to pull her back as ten razor sharp spears, five on each side, shot out the walls piercing the opposite side wall it sprang from. Sensei looked at Yuki as she spoke. "I might'a forgot about that little one."

He cringed his face. "Well lets try to remember the next one, agreed?"

Sensei let her lead the way around the corner. After intentionally triggering the next two traps they finally made it to an ancient combination tomb. Yuki tilted her head in confusion.

"This wasn't apart of the lesson." She stood dumb-founded.

Sensei stepped forward. "You only learn the part of the tomb when the previous Head teaches it to you. I can only do so from my death bed, Replica's rules or such events as these." He said as he began to spin the spindle.

Instead of three numbers, a six digit code was spun. When he finished with the code, the tomb lifted re-leasing the air that was trapped for so many years and creaked open.

Both Yuki and Sensei were temporarily blinded as the pure gold Soul Catcher shined and presented itself be-fore them. As their eyes adjusted a smile crept on Yuki's face.

"Wooooooow!" She was in awe.

CHAPTER 31

Walking closer Yuki extended her arm to grab it. As soon as her hand gripped the handle of it, almost instantly, the weapon began to wrap itself around her arm covering the length of her whole arm, becoming apart of her as if it was a limb.

If anyone was to see her looked like she had a gold extraterrestrial extension of an arm with a cannon blaster for a hand.

"Oh wow!" Yuki's eye's gleamed as she rotated her arm checking it out. "How am I supposed to get out of here with thing attached to me?"

Sensei walked toward her and pressed an invisible button on the contraption of the weapon and it detached falling to the ground as it shrank into a ornament. "Here, put it around your neck." Sensei demanded.

"There's no chain for it." Yuki held it up.

Sensei grabbed it and pressed it against her chest as a gold rope extended around her neck from the Soul Catcher. Leaving was easier than coming in. Making it back to the dinosaur exhibit, the kids still had the security busy. He even had an extra guard trying to help catch them as they ran circles in the area. Zionna was playing keep away with the guards hat while Ced. Jr. had a velvet rope swinging it every time the guard came into range.

Sensei kept walking as Yuki stopped at the scene surrounding her. "Hey! Hey kids! Come. Here!" They three of them froze in place at the tone of her voice.

The security turned toward Yuki. "Are these children with you?"

"Yes they are and I'll take it from here," She narrowed her eyes at them and clenched her teeth. "Lets. Go." They filed out one by one with their heads hung low. The officer dusted his hat off and headed back to his post with a strange feeling that he'd just missed something but shrugged the thought off and continued his day.

Stopping around the corner she paid them the rest of their stipend to which they happily accepted, then skipped off to really go with their parent who was oblivious to their actions.

"So now what?" Yuki turned to Sensei.

He didn't answer right away. He kept walking toward the exit where an escort awaited them. After they both sat and the car began to coast into traffic did Sensei finally answer.

"Time to Kill."

"So where are we headed? Do you have a location on the Lost Soul?"

"The Serengeti."

"Africa?"

"Hai."

"That's just great," Yuki sank in her seat. She wasn't a fan of the hot climate and would rather it been a different location.

"That's where the new distress call is coming from."

"What distress call! I don't know anything about any of this new found information you seem to have." She was becoming livid.

Her outburst didn't faze Sensei one bit, he looked out the window as he spoke. "It's alot you don't know. Knowledge is only transferred when it's your time to possess it. Too much knowledge is too much power. And the power of our knowledge is spread evenly so that Fate can happen as it suppose to. Your time will come for you to access the knowledge but I dread that day."

"So is this why you avoid Replica?"

"One of many reasons. Each visit there I seem to gain more responsibility. Like now! I'm just supposed to be training the next generation of Fate Seekers but replica doesn't think you're ready for certain knowledge so here I am. You must prove him wrong, Yuki. Do as he ask and you'll be rewarded." Sensei leaned back in his seat and closed his eyes. Yuki knew the meaning of the gesture.

Conversation over.

He passed her a cup. She drank its contents. Yuki blew a sigh and sank in her seat. She enjoyed the scenery as they were driven to the airport. Getting on the private jet, she drifted off into a nice sleep during the flight over the ocean.

Yuki's eyes began to flicker as strong winds swept her face waking her up in a panic. She began frantically looking around. "W-whats going on?"

The back hatch to the Jet laid flat exposing blue skies. Sensei was in front of Yuki putting the last strap around her when she finally started to put things together. "I know you didn't drug me!" She shouted over the loud winds. "Where are we, answer me right now!!"

Sensei grabbed a fist full of Yuki's shirt and pulled her close. "Silence! Listen, we are about to jump, and when we land I need you to be ready. Ethan is close." He released her and detached her seatbelt as well.

Yuki relaxed as she regained control of her breathing. Looking out the opening all she saw was blue skies and white clouds. The intercom made a beeping sound which meant an alert was to follow:

APPROACHING DROP ZONE T-MINUS THIRTY SECONDS...

Sensei stood at the edge holding the 'OH SHIT!' bar that was welded on the side of the aircraft as he looked out awaiting the final countdown. Yuki stood beside him. The chime came again:

5...4...3...2...1...

GO! GO! GO!

Simultaneously they jumped and let the air guide them through the sky. Yuki experienced plenty of simulated flight jumps but this was the first actual real experience. Sensei watched her all gradually transform into a controlled glide as the lessons came to use.

The ground began to get closer as the ant-like figures became physical and recognizable structures of land. Wildlife ran across the terrain, the birds flew in flocks tree to tree in search of rest stops because of the distance between each one was kilometers of grasslands.

The sight had Yuki in awe as she pulled the cord that released her parachute and coasted to the surface. Sensei and Yuki landed a few kilometers in front of a pride of lioness and their cubs feasting on the carcass of a gazelle. Releasing the parachute from their person they headed east when a cool chill blew their way.

"Stop! You feel that?" Sensei pointed to the air. Yuki was hot but smiled after the draft hit her.

"It feels good, especially with this thousand degree weather." She exaggerated.

The draft felt like a winter breeze. It made the grass stiffen for a while as the heat gave it its wave back. "This way! Hurry." Sensei took off in a sprint that left a dust trail. Yuki turned around to see a lioness closing in on her. Her eyes bubbled before she took off in a sprint headed toward Sensei leaving the lioness in the rearview.

They ran for miles until Sensei abruptly stopped in his tracks with a fifteen foot slide and Yuki did the same three seconds behind. He scanned the area. "He's here."

Everything appeared the same in all directions. Blue skies and greenish brown grass everywhere. That look was only for the human eye. Through Sensei eye's he could see every living organism on the ground and beneath it.

Between the tall grass he spotted Ethan feasting on a lions corpse. Sensei slowly turned toward Yuki and whispered. "Get the Soul Catcher and --"

Before Sensei could finish his statement, an extended fist came across his face sending him flying backward. Ethan gave a demonic chuckle. "I knew I smelled death," Yuki tried to grab for her necklace but was also punched and forced to drop the Soul Catcher as she flew in the opposite direction. "Uh, uh, not this time."

Ethan stood twelve feet and bent his body in attempt to grab the miniature Soul Catcher that couldn't be wielded by a human or any lost soul, only a Fate Seeker could have that honor.

Dropping the weapon instantly after it pierced his skin he took a few steps back. Sensei was closing in after he recovered from his attack. Ethan didn't even see him as Sensei brandished a sword disconnecting Ethan's arm from his shoulder.

He winced in pain as it fell to the ground. With his free hand he backslapped Sensei sending him flipping to the dirt. Ethan turned around to see Yuki on approach as his wound leaked black blood the color of oil like a faucet. She was closing in quickly but not fast enough when Ethan grabbed his limb from the ground, held it in its place as he inhaled a huge breath of Earth's elements.

"Yeesssss!" He growled as his arm re attached itself also rejuvenating him.

Yuki came into reaching distance just in time to receive a huge kick to her chest knocking her in a different direction. Luckily she landed where she needed to be. She slowly pulled her body up and looked to her left where the Soul Catcher sparkled as it reflected off the sun.

Picking the weapon up, it attached itself to her entire arm and was ready to shoot. Turning around Yuki noticed Ethan had Sensei in the air with his feet dangling as he choked him. "S-shoot him!!" He tried to fight from the air.

Yuki aimed her arm and it powered up to the max. There was no trigger. Confusion was evident. "How do I shoot it!" She yelled.

"Tell it with your mind!!!!"

Ethan turned toward Yuki as she closed her eyes and commanded the Soul Catcher to fire. It spit out a fierce blue plasma that attacked the flesh of Ethan and started deteriorating him as it spread causing him to drop to his knees and then released Sensei who fell holding his throat gasping for air.

Ethan made an attempt to inhale the dirt, but it was useless because Yuki never released the thought in her mind and the plasma blast continued to fire until Ethan's body turned to dust and his soul was sucked into the Soul Catcher.

"That was easy enough, eh." Sensei brush himself off. He looked to the sky and then all around. "How are we going to get back to civilization from the Mother's Land Serengeti."

Yuki smiled. "Call an U.ber."

Sensei looked confused. "A what!?"

CHAPTER 32

Solo and Sarang drove in silence. Both watched different sceneries play out in their minds. Solo sat in the passenger seat with heavy thoughts. the new found information that Yuki had plans on killing him had him ready to get it however it came. He told himself that getting caught with his pants down was never an option. Running for sure wasn't one either.

All his life he attacked any problem head on. The next destination was where their current problem rested.

The Fate Seeker's Estate.

The thought of walking in the mansion with ill intentions forced Solo's skin to get rigid like a croc'. His eyes widened at the sight of it. Sarang noticed the change as well. "When did you learn that?" He shrugged. "Man-nn, I didn't. Shit be changin' everyday it seems. I think I'm bionic or some shit. What you think?"

Sarang turned her eyes to the road without a response. Solo's skin returned normal. In the back of his mind he wondered why Yuki wanted him dead. He didn't tell anyone about his abilities, he completed every Calling that she assigned without any flaws. Solo racked his brain for an answer that never came.

Sarang read his thoughts and shook her head. "She don't need a reason. She feels threatened."

"By me?" Solo didn't believe that one bit. "I aint nobody, shit, I'm the same as you," He said not knowing the depth of the comparison. "The difference is that maybe I'm better looking than you, but that's not my fault that you was beat with an ugly stick."

Never taking her eye's off the road she punched him in the arm. He instantly started rubbing where it connected. "You punch like a girl but look like a man."

Nearing the Estate, Solo's mind wandered to thoughts of Onyx and Teddy. Did they play a role in Yuki's sudden change of heart? What he didn't know was that the answer to all his questions sat across from him.

Sarang.

Sarang was the main reason but not "the" reason. There were plenty, one being Replica wanting to meet him, Sensei informing her that Replica felt she was not ready to obtain important information and the fact that

Solo was progressing rapidly and much faster than she ever did.

Jealousy was the reason why his demise was etched in stone by the leader of the Fate Seekers. Still, he had no clue.

Sarang had a few reasons why she wanted to attack. Love, betrayal, deceit and much more was the fluid that fueled her fire. the lie she lived was over, she couldn't brush the facts under the carpet. that person that caused so much pain had to go. That was her final testament.

Driving up the pathway leading to the Estate, a nervous chill went down the spine of Solo that resembled a wave of his spinal cord as each bone rose and fell back into place. Sarang glanced at Solo, "You ready?"

"Uuhh, this what we, uhh, want to do, right?" She stared daggers at him. "I'm just askin', you know my momma aint raise no punk but damn. It's a lot of pretty killers in there and you know I'm not suppose to be hittin' no girls."

She curled her lips at the statement, then rolled her eyes and smiled. "If you plan on getting anymore of me, you better get--"

"Ok, ok, you win. You aint even gotta act like that. Life without that," He nodded to her crotch area, "is a life not worth living."

"Boy shut up and come on."

Her once innocent vibes were long gone. Time with Solo aged her in his urban culture. Even her choice of clothes changed from cheap or average to boogie and

---

expensive. When they stepped out the car she exited the car in a custom North face fitted one piece jumper with Teflon etched in the fabric. Her hair was braided back in four French braids with her natural hair.

On her hip she held two .40 caliber Glocks and an M4 assault rifle hung from her shoulder. Solo had a similar attire except his was a two tone piece top and bottom. They climbed the stairs. The maid had wide eyes when she opened the door.

"Daijobu?"

Sarang smiled. "Hai, we're fine but I think you should take the rest of the day."

"Nande?" She asked (what), not understanding why she was asked to leave.

Solo walked beside her placing a hand on her shoulder then waved his rifle. "Sayonara."

Recognition hit. "Wakarimashta," She nodded her understanding. "Arigato." She nodded thanking them then swiftly ran down the multiple steps holding her skirt so she wouldn't trip. Solo smiled at Sarang. "She was nice, right."

Sarang entered and stood in the middle of the foyer with a position where she could see all angles of the estate and its many hallways. She looked to the ceiling.

"Konbanwa!!" She sang a boastful evening greeting.

There was complete silence. The only sound that could be heard was the wind blowing as if they were still outside. Sarang and Solo took positions back to back.

The it happened.

Looking up, six Seekers seemed to be flying as they leaped over the balcony in sync toward Sarang. She raised her rifle and fired as Solo turned to face the action and shot the remaining two that weren't hit.

All six bodies landed with a loud thud. Before they knew it, the heel of the other seekers attacked their spinal cords sending them flying forward toward a wall as they dropped the assault rifles.

The two Seekers picked the weapons up and fired them rapidly at Sarang and Solo as they ran to avoid the shots. They dived into the dining room area and quickly took refuge against the wall. Sarang looked at Solo then slapped him hard on his cheek.

"Ouch! What was that for?" He rubbed his cheek.

"You was supposed to have the backside."

"My bad, players fuck up too, plus them broads came out of nowhere."

She rolled her eyes, "Ugh!" Then dived to the opposite side as shots barely missed her. With both their backs pressed against the wall they locked eyes. Solo blew a kiss and pulled his two handguns out and fired at the two Seekers who returned fire hitting Solo all in his chest sending him flying back in the room.

Sarang shook her head. "Dummy."

He looked at her."Bae, I-I can see the light."

"Boy shut up and get out the way before they get a lucky shot off!" She leaned around shooting her twin Glocks.

The bullets that hit Solo were absorbed by the Fate Land's version of Teflon that was ten times stronger than Earths. The bullets however still had the pain and had Solo squirming. He was winded but managed to crawl out the way.

Sarang fired controlled shots finally hitting both of the Seekers.

"Come on, Solo, we have to go upstairs and find her."

He staggered to his feet, "I'm waiting on you."

Scaling the wall quietly as possible, both on opposite sides of the stairwell, they headed to the next floor. Picking up a piece of shattered glass, Solo used it as a mirror to look around the corner and down the hall.

As soon as the view became focus on a target, a sharp dagger knocked it out his hand shattering its remains into small pieces. "Shit! Almost sliced my fingers off!"

Sarang looked over at him. "How many?"

Solo glanced at his hand. "I'm good, all of them intact."

"No, Stupid! How many Seekers down the hall?"

"Oh, it's four left...I think."

"Lets go!"

Sarang sprang from around the wall and shot her twin Glocks as she ran on the side of the walls dodging different type of knives thrown her way. Solo ran straight, no wall action for him, instead of alluding the daggers he shot them out the air as they spun.

Closing in, the knives ceased to fly and their clips were empty. There were two Seekers left and three laid lifeless in the hall. Solo and Sarang stood toe to toe with the remaining two. One of them spoke with a side grin. "I knew you was a mistake." She narrowed her eyes at Sarang. She frowned knowing that everybody knew more about her than she did herself.

Screaming, Sarang threw a punch that connected with the Seeker's chin that sent her backward.

Solo's eyes got big as he watched the Seeker fly back. "Dayum'! You hit her hard as shit-"

A fist across his own chin shut him up sending him in the opposite direction of the Seeker that Sarang hit. The last Seeker turned toward Sarang and began to fight each other.

They exchanged blows one after another as Solo began to get up. He shook himself off, "Damn, Shawty hit me hard as shit." He felt his jaw and was satisfied that it was still attached. Narrowing his eyes, he noticed the other Seeker headed toward Sarang. His emotion forced his fist to swell and multiply in size as he ran toward her. After a few strides he was across the room swinging a super-sized punch that sent the seeker through a window.

Running to the window, he saw the seeker looking like a shiskkabob as her back arched through a light pole. Sarang continued to fight the remaining seeker as Solo began to watch.

He was mesmerized when different articles of clothing began to get ripped off.

Sarang caught glimpse of him. "Really?"

"What!? You got it, right." He asked.

Sarang dodged a punch and countered with a punch of her own and added a spinning heel kick that sent the seeker's face through the corner of an old mahogany table leaving her body propped on her knees.

"See, I told you." Solo grinned.

Walking through the halls, the maids and other workers scrambled to safety not understanding what was going on. The both of them made it to the living quarters after checking every other possibility. There they stood at Yuki's favorite location, the spa.

Solo was about to knock until Sarang kicked the double doors wide open. Entering the room it was empty. it had a dark gloom to it as they looked around. The air was moist as the walls sweated. Yuki sat on a throne-like chair facing the both of them. Everything in the room seemed to be lined against the wall out the way in preparation for this very moment.

"So my children wish to take my throne," Yuki started in a soft voice that gradually raised. "THEY WISH TO DETHRONE ME!!" She stood.

Sarang took a step forward and Solo grabbed her arm as she spoke. "IM NOT YOUR CHILD! You stole my life and now, it's time for me to end yours."

Yuki chuckled. That only added more fury to the assault Sarang mapped out in her head. Yuki looked at Solo, "Is this how you feel too..after all the gifts I've gifted to you. I've made you a GOD amongst peasants!"

He rubbed his chin. "Welllll, you kinda' did a dick move by putting me on your lil death list. The why, I still don't know, but I'm kinda like on Sarang's side on this one."

She grinned. " Then you'll both die." She said barely above a whisper.

In lightening speed, Yuki was on her second assault before Sarang had the chance to get in her stance watching solo fly through the door they came through. Sarang blocked Yuki's next assault aimed at her. the power the blow sent Sarang in a slide of a few feet.

Yuki's skin began to ridge as her eyes darkened with yellow slits. Sarang's eyes did the same but her skin remained blemish free. Yuki attacked throwing multiple combinations that Sarang couldn't handle as her face began to swell from the multiple connected punches and kicks. Solo finally gained his legs from under himself and rushed Yuki with his oversized fist.

She ducked his attempts then punched him in his ribs cracking a couple of them as he groaned in agony. Sarang jumped on her neck from the blind side and was tossed off not before she grabbed the Soul Catcher necklace from off Yuki's neck unbeknownst to her.

Sarang opened her hand from the ground and noticed the chain glow bright. Solo was on his feet prepared to attack when Sarang threw the chain at him,

"Here!" She screamed. "Use this."

Yuki tried to grab it out the air but missed landing on her side. it landed in Solo's palm and began to bond with him on a cellular level covering his whole arm. It looked like a golden cannon with a muzzle and wide air holes.

His eye's bubbled with awe. "Now what!?"

"Shoot it!!!" Sarang yelled from the ground wincing in pain. Yuki ran toward Solo as he lifted the Soul Catcher that was now his arm.

'SHOOT IT?' He thought in his head questioning the mechanics of the weapon, but the thought acted as a command and initiated a blue fiery blast that attacked Yuki's body as she tried to fight the plasma that spread over her body while she still approached Solo.

Yuki proved to be no match for the Soul Catcher when she fell to a knee and her rigid scales began to boil into blisters then exploded. her remains went in every which direction. Solo lowered the weapon as he grabbed his chest. his heart was beating rapidly.

Sarang lifted her head and stood excitedly then ran to Solo jumping in his embrace. "You did it!!"

He gave her a slight smile then everything went black as he collapsed in her arms.

Riley tip toed into Solo's bedroom with a cup of water grinning. He froze in place when he heard the screech of his mother. "Solo!!" His shoulders rose from the sound, cringing his body.

Solo's eyes flickered, but he remained in a deep sleep as he wiped the slob off his mouth. Slowly his eyes began to open and he noticed Riley smiling hard.

"Good morning, Punk!" Riley tossed the contents of the cup into Solo's face then hightailed it out the room. He rose up quickly wiping his face and stretched after he realized it was water. He stood up, the bedroom looked different to him. He paid the minor changes no mind as he walked to the bathroom.

Washing his face he collected his thoughts when Valerie came bursting through the door with an old suit in her hand. "Here, I just ironed it for you. I don't want you having any excuses for being late to your interview."

It was pressed to his chest and he grabbed it confused. "Interview?!"

"Yes, interview. I set you up one downtown. It's a labor job so hurry up!" He was so confused and was lost for words when she continued. "Just because you just finished school and don't want to go to college don't mean you just going to lounge around here."

"I got a job, Ma."

"The hell you do, but what I do know is you got fifteen minutes to get up out this house. I'm about to take Riley to school."

Before he could answer she walked off. Solo hurried and washing his face. He tried to find his phone, but it was missing. The calendar on his wall was off by months. He ran to the house phone and dialed a number expecting it to be disconnected but it wasn't.

Ebony's cell phone rang twice before he hung it up. "Am I goin' crazy? I know that shit couldn't had been no damn dream. Was it?!" He looked in his top drawer inside a pair of socks and found his stash of drugs. The same stash of drugs that he had the day before he met Yuki.

He let out a sigh. "It was a dream," He sat on his bed. "but it felt so real. Damn, I gotta stop smokin'." He shook his head and began putting on his suit. After getting dressed, he came downstairs to an empty house. The only thing in the house was breakfast on the stove and a note:

ENJOY BREAKFAST AND DON'T
BE LATE!!!

On top of the stove was some loose cash. he grabbed it and counted. It was the exact same amount that Valerie gave him in his dream. Secretly he wished the dream was real but after eating he realized it wasn't.

Walking to the corner he tried to flag a cab. It was a nearly impossible task in his neighborhood. Still he stood in hopes of a willing driver. His eyes widened when a tinted Lincoln pulled along side him.

He backed up expecting to see Yuki but when the window lowered and a beautiful woman sat in the back seat that wasn't her, his jaw dropped.

"Sarang?" Confusion and shock was evident.

"Yea, Boy, get in. Did you miss me?" She smirked.

"H-How did--" His mind was everywhere.

"Get in, I'll tell you everything on the way to talk to Replica in the Fate Lands. We need to discuss the new world order as the new Heads of the Seekers."

He smiled tossing his clip on tie to the curb and jumped in the car.

The End.

ABOUT THE AUTHOR

Cedric Spicer is the author of two great novels. (Surviving the Killzone) and (Blueface Dreams). He enjoys writing and often draws as a hobby. He is from the District of Columbia, our nations capital. For more information and contact visit his social media sites.

Facebook: Cedric Spicer (DroPak Da Author)
Instagram: @dro_pak 2.0